'Do not wor

'All of us have
along in our li
gently, 'and it i

Still Pauline could not speak, and she tried
to take a deep breath to steady herself. His
hands rested on her in a warm and protective
hold, and, although her back was towards
him, she caught the tang of his aftershave—
a spicy fragrance that blended with the heady
masculinity that surrounded him like an aura,
and of which she had been aware at their very
first meeting. Was it only that morning? It
seemed so much longer.

Margaret Holt trained as a nurse and midwife in Surrey, and has practised midwifery for thirty-five years. She moved to Manchester when she married, and has two graduate daughters. Now widowed, she enjoys writing, reading, gardening and supporting her church. Margaret believes strongly in smooth and close co-operation between obstetrician and midwife for the safe care of mothers and their babies.

Recent titles by the same author:

AN INDISPENSABLE WOMAN
A SONG FOR DR ROSE
A MIDWIFE'S CHOICE
A PLACE OF REFUGE

REMEDY FOR PRIDE

BY

MARGARET HOLT

To dear Marie,
with love and all
good wishes from
Margaret Holt
xx

Christmas 1995

MILLS & BOON

For the Trafford Midwives

*MILLS & BOON, the Rose Device and
LOVE ON CALL are trademarks of the publisher.
Harlequin Mills & Boon Limited,
Eton House, 18-24 Paradise Road, Richmond, Surrey TW9 1SR
This edition published by arrangement with Harlequin Enterprises B.V.*

© Margaret Holt 1996

ISBN 0 263 79458 X

*Set in Times 10 on 12 pt. by
Rowland Phototypesetting Limited
Bury St Edmunds, Suffolk*

03-9601-491205

*Made and printed in Great Britain
Cover illustration by George Noble*

CHAPTER ONE

'WELL done, Joanna, love—your baby's properly fixed on now, and sucking away like fury, bless him!'

Sister Pauline Stephens pushed back a limp strand of corn-coloured hair from her flushed face and gave a smile of encouragement to the breast-feeding mother, though Mrs Joanna Sandrini's condition two days after Caesarean section was giving cause for some anxiety. Her temperature was up and her pulse was racing, but the most alarming sign was her distended tummy and constant nausea. She was determined to breast-feed her baby son Antonio—called Toni for short—but, much as midwife Pauline admired Joanna's insistence on giving him the ideal food, she was becoming increasingly concerned about his mother.

'Just lie back on the pillows, Jo, and let me hold Toni while he has his dinner!' she instructed. 'That's right, young man, you've soon learned what to do, haven't you?'

The two women exchanged indulgent smiles over the baby's downy head, though Mrs Sandrini's face was drawn and toxic-looking. She winced as Toni fastened his hard little gums to her tender nipple, and ran her dry tongue around her lips; she did not utter a word of complaint. Pauline's back ached from leaning over the bed and cradling the baby in her arms to keep his weight off his mother's tense abdomen, but she too would not have dreamed of voicing her discomfort.

She had asked the obstetric house officer to come

and see Mrs Sandrini as soon as the morning's gynaecology operation list was completed, but the delivery
unit was hectically busy, and as the postnatal ward was
not looked upon as a priority there was no sign yet of
a white coat. Pauline decided to ring the gynae theatre
again as soon as Toni's feed was finished.

At that moment the bed-curtains parted and a flustered nursing auxiliary poked her head through
the gap.

'Dr Ghiberti's here, Sister.'

'Dr who?' Pauline did not recognise the name.

'From the surgical team, Sister. He says he's been
asked to see Mrs Sandrini.'

'Oh, I see. Is he in the ward office?'

'No, Sister, I am here. Good morning!'

Pauline drew in a sharp breath as soon as she saw the
tall man who silently appeared and towered above the
auxiliary. Just for a split-second she thought,
Giorgio!—for he had the same arrestingly dark eyes,
above which long black brows almost met above his
nose. But Giorgio had not had such a lofty nose, long,
straight and symmetrical—the type of nose that Pauline
supposed would be called patrician. His dark, wavy
hair was just long enough to reach the collar of his
white coat. Pauline quickly returned his greeting.

'Good morning, Doctor. I didn't quite catch
your——'

'Ghiberti, Sister.' He glanced from the midwife to
the mother and raised a questioning eyebrow. 'Mrs
Sandrini, yes?' he asked, in a deep, attractively
accented voice. His mouth was generously wide,
revealing strong white teeth. The classic Latin type,
thought Pauline, remembering the Italian holiday two
years ago with her friend Jenny, when she had met

and fallen for Giorgio. But this was no time for reminiscences.

'Yes, Dr Ghiberti. Mrs Sandrini had an emergency Caesarean section on March twenty-seventh for antepartum haemorrhage at thirty-eight weeks. First baby.'

As Pauline reeled off the facts she gently removed the baby from his mother and held him against her shoulder. 'This morning she was unable to tolerate anything by mouth, though she should be on light diet by now, and she feels nauseated. Her temperature, pulse and blood pressure chart is there at the foot of the bed. Her urethral catheter was removed twenty-four hours after operation, and intravenous fluids discontinued as per routine.'

He examined the chart and nodded to Joanna, who smiled wanly.

'You are not drinking water, Mrs Sandrini, no?'

'No, Doctor, I can't keep it down,' sighed Joanna, and as Toni gave a loud and satisfying burp over Pauline's shoulder his mother also belched painfully with the trapped wind in her stomach.

'Oh, I beg your pardon,' she apologised miserably. 'Is it normal to feel so bloated and uncomfortable?'

'No, but don't worry, my dear,' said the doctor sympathetically, replacing the chart and taking his stethoscope out of his pocket. 'Let me listen to your tummy, please.'

Pauline placed the happily glassy-eyed Toni in his cot, and pulled back the duvet. The doctor took his time, placing the instrument over different areas. He gently touched the operation incision, held together with skin-clips, and asked Pauline for a glove and lubricant to perform a rectal examination. He looked at Joanna's tongue, and asked her a few more questions, after which he nodded and folded away the stethoscope.

'*Parli italiano, Signora Sandrini?*' he asked with a smile.

'*Si, dottore, benché sono inglese. Mio marito è italiano,*' she replied in pleased surprise.

Pauline remembered enough of the Italian she had studied to know that Mrs Sandrini had said that she was English and married to an Italian; she resisted the temptation to venture a sentence or two herself, there being far more pressing matters on her mind—such as what was to be done about Joanna's non-functioning bowel. She was only too aware of the dangers of paralytic ileus, which could cause a total stoppage after any major abdominal surgery.

'Do not worry, *signora,*' the doctor repeated. 'We shall get your tummy working again, and first we must recommence the drip because you cannot drink fluids. Then Sister will pass a thin tube down into your stomach—the feel of it going through your nose may not be too comfortable, but it will bring great relief to your tummy, I promise.'

He turned to Pauline. '*Allora,* Sister, we shall talk in the office now, please?'

'Back in a few minutes, Joanna,' she said, and went ahead of him to the postnatal ward office. Anticipating his instructions, she set out on the desk request forms for a full blood count, urea and electrolyte levels, blood and urine cultures and antibiotic sensitivities.

'We shall have to keep her on a drip and gastric suction until we hear normal bowel sounds again,' he said wryly, turning down the corners of his mouth. 'Poor girl! I will start her on a course of broad spectrum antibiotics—ampicillin and flagyl—to be given six-hourly. I would also like her to have a stat dose of omnopon, twenty milligrams for her pain, to be repeated six-hourly as necessary.'

Pauline nodded, feeling really sorry for Joanna, but knowing that this regime was likely to be effective.

'And, of course, she is not in a fit condition to feed the child,' he went on. 'Your staff will give him bottles for the next twenty-four hours or so, yes?'

'*No*, Doctor.' Pauline's reply was definite. 'Joanna is particularly insistent on feeding her baby, and would be distressed if not allowed to do so. She will be given constant assistance from a midwife throughout each feed. We are firm promoters of breast-feeding here, Doctor.'

He looked up from his seat at the desk, his deep-set eyes narrowing slightly.

'In that case, I would prefer that you express the milk from her and give it to the child in a bottle.'

Pauline's mouth, usually curved upward in a ready smile, now straightened into an unyielding line. Her voice was ominously quiet as she replied.

'And *I* would prefer to abide by the mother's wishes, Dr Ghiberti. I will see that all your orders regarding her surgical condition are carried out as soon as possible, but, as regards her postnatal routine, *I* am in charge.'

His black eyebrows shot up, and his expression showed quite clearly that he was not used to being contradicted by nursing staff.

'Indeed, Sister? And may I be permitted to ask what is your qualification for taking charge of the patient I have been specially asked to see and advise on?'

'Certainly you may ask, Doctor. I am a registered midwife—a practitioner in my own right. I suggest that you keep to your speciality and I will keep to mine, all right?'

There was a long pause while Pauline held her breath, wondering if she had gone too far. Was it only that he reminded her of faithless Giorgio? Or was it his arrogance, the impression he gave that every woman he met must be bowled over by his Latin good looks? If so, she would be the exception!

Still seated at the desk, he looked up at her appraisingly.

'*Mi scusi*, Sister, may I ask your name? And how long you have worked on this ward?'

The dark eyes searched her face and a tiny tremor ran through her whole body—not unpleasurably. There was definitely something about the man she found oddly disturbing, and the fact annoyed her.

'Sister Pauline Stephens,' she answered briskly. 'I have worked here in the maternity department for the past two years, ever since I qualified as a midwife. For the past ten months I have been junior midwifery sister on the post natal ward.'

'And you are a registered nurse also?' he enquired.

'Yes, most of the midwives are. I did all my training here at Beltonshaw General Hospital,' she informed him. 'And now, Dr Ghiberti, would you care to tell me *your* qualifications, and why you left Italy to come and work in a Manchester suburban hospital?'

A faint gleam of humour lit his eyes.

'Certainly. Niccolo Ghiberti, doctor of medicine, graduate of the University of Florence. I am here on an exchange scheme, to occupy the position of surgical registrar on the team of Mr Mason, whose work on alimentary cancer has received much acclaim. Will that be sufficient, Sister Stephens?'

'Yes, thank you, Dr Ghiberti,' she replied politely, thinking how unexciting her own history sounded by comparison. 'And now, if you'll excuse me, I must attend to Mrs Sandrini.'

'Of course. If you wish I can take the blood samples while I am here.'

'No, that won't be necessary. I take blood samples all the time.'

'Indeed? But if I put up the IV drip I can take the bloods at the same time, and save Joanna having two needles in her arm.'

He was right, though Pauline had not expected a surgeon of registrar status to be willing to do a houseman's duties on Maternity. As there was still no sign of any member of the obstetric team she accepted his offer, and hurried to assemble the drip set—plastic litre bags of glucose and saline solution, syringes, needles and adhesive dressings.

On the bottom of the trolley she placed a gastric suction tube in its sterile package, with lubricating jelly and paper skin-tape. She added a large aspirating syringe and a plastic spigot to plug the free end of the tube. Poor Joanna! But Pauline knew that gastric suction would ease the horrid sensation of nausea, and after twenty-four hours or so of complete rest the inert alimentary canal would gradually start its normal movement again.

It was at times like this that Pauline was thankful for her general training. She had worked as a staff nurse on a women's surgical ward after qualifying, and then spent six months in the general theatres, where the work demanded a high standard of technical expertise. Nevertheless, she had missed the personal contact with patients. When she had embarked on mid-

wifery training, after the holiday in Italy, she had found
that her relationship with the mothers satisfied this
need—plus, of course, her contact with the babies,
which she adored. Now that Sister Beddows of Postnatal was due to retire, Pauline had put in an
application for her post. At twenty-six she felt it was
time to make a decision about her career, and as a
local girl, brought up in Beltonshaw where she still
lived contentedly with her widowed mother, it seemed
an obvious next step to take.

When Dr Ghiberti had finished putting up the intravenous line on Mrs Sandrini, and Pauline had
established gastric suction, he checked the first dose
of antibiotics with her. She was impressed by his deft
and seemingly effortless method of working, and his
air of easy friendliness with Joanna. Even so, it was
just as well that he was not on the obstetric team, she
decided. She would not have cared to have him around
frequently, disturbing the all-female atmosphere of
Maternity with his Mediterranean looks!

Or would she? This unexpected meeting with
Ghiberti had set her thoughts off on a nostalgic trip
back to the holiday she and Jenny had spent in Italy,
visiting Rome and Venice. They had fallen in love with
the country in general—and with Riccardo and Giorgio
in particular.

In Jenny's case romance had blossomed, and had
led to marriage with Dr Riccardo Alberi and a completely new way of life, but Giorgio had not kept his
promise to stay in touch with Pauline, and her elation
had turned to bitter disappointment and heartbreak.

Swept off her feet by his incredible lovemaking,
Pauline had simply not believed that his desire for her
could have been less real and lasting than the kind of

emotions he had stirred in her. When her letters and telephone calls had remained unanswered and ignored she had experienced the worst weeks of her life, and since then had not had any serious relationships.

And now this Niccolo had suddenly appeared out of the blue, reminding her of that interlude and stirring up oddly similar sensations in her heart as when she had first met Giorgio. . .

She wondered how Jenny and Riccardo were getting on these days. They ran a small private hospital near Fiesole in Tuscany, and Pauline had a standing invitation to visit them. So far she had not found the time to accept it, and now that she was about to take up a senior sister's post it seemed unlikely that she would ever get to the Clinico Silverio. She had an interview that very afternoon with Mrs Gresham, the midwifery superintendent, but that would only be a formality, and Pauline smiled to herself in anticipation of her new appointment.

'But—but I don't understand, Mrs Gresham. When I was made junior sister on Postnatal you told me I'd be next in line when Sister Beddows retired.'

Pauline's incredulous dismay was reflected in her voice as much as in the wide blue-grey eyes that stared back at the superintendent. Mrs Gresham glanced sideways at Mr Hawke, the newly appointed manager for Obstetrics and Gynaecology. He in turn gave Pauline an apologetic smile that frankly infuriated her.

'It's like this, Miss Stephens. We have to work within a very tight budget, as I'm sure you must realise. So many maternity cases are discharged home early now, and it's changed the whole concept of the postnatal ward.'

Pauline wondered how an accountant like Hawke could possibly understand the concept of any special-ised field in nursing, postnatal work included.

'And because of this rapid turnover of cases we are dispensing with the post of junior sister on Postnatal, and employing an extra staff-midwife instead.'

'But when Sister Beddows retires you'll still need a senior sister, surely?' asked Pauline, addressing Mrs Gresham.

'Ah, that's just it, you see,' answered Mr Hawke, putting his fingertips together like a headmaster deal-ing with a not very bright pupil. 'We simply haven't the resources to take on another full-time midwife on a G-grade salary, so we're looking for an older and perhaps more suitable midwife at F-grade. Sister Pen-rose has been a community midwife for many years, but she's beginning to find the night-driving a bit much for her now, and wants to take a hospital post for her last few years of employment. She's happy to continue on an F-grade salary, and——'

'And so am I, if you can't afford me otherwise!' interrupted Pauline, flushing indignantly. 'I hope you haven't got the impression that dealing with newly delivered mothers and their babies is an easy option—it can be anything but!'

She was totally taken aback by the way this interview was going. Sister Beddows had personally recom-mended her as her successor, but it seemed that the appointment was a foregone conclusion.

Mrs Gresham saw the expression on Pauline's face, and hastily cut in.

'I'm terribly sorry, Pauline—believe me. The NHS is under terrific financial pressure, and resources are stretched to the limit. Our circumstances here at

Beltonshaw are very different now from when you first qualified. If you only knew the difficulties of juggling with available staffing levels, I think you'd probably come to realise that I—that is, Mr Hawke and I—have made the best decision over Sister Penrose. Now, what I want to tell you about is a vacancy for a midwifery sister on night duty coming up later this year. It's currently F-grade, but if you decided to take it on for a year or two I could almost guarantee—— Pauline, what's the matter? Are you all right?'

Pauline had risen to her feet. She found that she was shaking all over.

'Thank you, Mrs Gresham, but I didn't come here to apply for a night sister's job. I'm only interested in the post for which I have been specially recommended. Obviously I've been under a false impression.'

'Now, don't be silly, dear,' began Mr Hawke soothingly, but Pauline ignored him.

'My notice of termination of contract will be on your desk this evening, Mrs Gresham. Good afternoon.'

'Pauline, *please*, you mustn't think of leaving us!' the superintendent almost wailed.

'Don't worry, there are plenty of newly qualified midwives out there looking for jobs,' replied the failed applicant as she went out of the door.

Mrs Stephens was genuinely upset to hear her daughter's disappointing news that afternoon.

'It's too bad of them, Pauline, and just as that article in the paper said last week! The NHS is run by non-medical, non-nursing accountants who treat the patients as consumer units with no thought for them as people, nor for the staff. But Pauline, dear, what will you do now?'

'I shall have to think about it, Mum. I might go back to surgical nursing, or do a bit of theatre staffing if there's a job going,' replied Pauline dejectedly.

Her mother came over and sat beside her on the settee in the living-room of their modest semi. To Pauline's surprise she felt her hand clasped and held while Mrs Stephens searched for words.

'The fact is, dear, I'm especially sorry to hear about this setback in your career just now, because—well, I have got some news too, you see.'

'What do you mean, Mum?' demanded Pauline, forgetting her own problems in sudden alarm. 'Is there something that I should know about? Tell me at once!'

Still holding her daughter's hand, Helen Stephens drew a deep breath.

'It's nothing to worry about, Pauline. It's wonderful news for me, and I just hope and pray that you'll think so too.' She spoke with a shy awkwardness that Pauline had never heard before.

'Go on, Mum, I can take it.'

'All right, then. Dr Stafford has asked me to marry him.'

'Mother! And will you?' asked Pauline, open-mouthed.

'Yes, Pauline. We're both widowed and rather lonely, and we have quite a lot in common,' replied Helen, looking down at their clasped hands.

'But he's our GP!'

'Well, exactly, dear. We've known each other for years, and since he lost Enid he's been coming to church with me sometimes and giving me lifts and—— Oh, it's all happened so naturally—we both realised it at the same time, and—— Do wish us joy, Pauline, I couldn't bear it if you didn't. You mustn't feel that I love you any less because of Graham.'

Her eyes shone with her new-found happiness as she pleaded for her daughter's approval, and Pauline hastened to reassure her.

'Of course I'm happy for you, Mum, only it's such a—a complete surprise. You'll have to give me time to take it in.'

She hesitated just for a moment, then turned and flung her arms around Helen in a warm hug.

'Congratulations, love,' she murmured a little shakily. 'If it's what you want, I'm thrilled for you and Dr Stafford—er, Graham.'

'Bless you, Pauline, that means so much to me,' whispered Helen gratefully. 'And I just hope that things work out for you at the hospital. You know that you'll always have a home with Graham and me for as long as you need one—that goes without saying.'

'Thanks, Mum, I know.' Pauline managed a smile, but had already decided that she would have to find somewhere else to live in these changed circumstances. Her future now appeared very uncertain indeed.

At five o'clock Pauline returned to the ward and took the report from the staff-midwife who had covered the afternoon shift. As soon as the hand-over was completed she hurried to Mrs Sandrini's bedside, and was relieved to find her patient looking a little better and no longer feeling nauseated.

'I can't thank you enough, Pauline—I only wish I could take you home with me,' said Joanna weakly.

'Go away with you—it's only my job,' smiled Pauline. 'Now, are you still adamant about feeding him yourself, or——?'

'Of course! And I think he's ready for me again,'

replied Joanna, looking towards the cot, from which impatient squeaks could be heard.

'Right, I'll just check your temp and blood pressure, and then I'll change our young man before his feed. Let's see—it's the left side this time, isn't it?'

When Toni had been fed and tucked down again, Pauline checked the six o'clock dose of antibiotics with a student midwife. As she drew up the freshly mixed solution into a syringe a deep voice spoke behind her shoulder and made her start.

'For Mrs Sandrini, Sister Stephens?'

Pauline spun round. 'Good evening, Dr Ghiberti. Yes, she's just finished feeding her baby, and I'm giving her this now, plus another injection of omnopon.'

'Good. Is she better? May I see her?'

When he had spoken with Joanna, and studied her temperature and fluid balance chart, he gently felt her tummy and nodded encouragement.

'Well done. Tomorrow we shall see much improvement, I'm sure.' He looked into the cot and put a finger to his lips. 'Sleeping like a Botticelli angel, so let me not disturb him. May I have her case-notes, Sister? No, do not worry about fetching them; I will come to the office.'

Seated at the desk, he wrote a few observations on the patient's progress, then, closing the folder, he sat back and regarded Pauline. She found his dark penetrating eyes disconcerting.

'And you, Sister Pauline?' he asked. 'Have *you* had a good day? I saw you returning to the hospital this evening, battling against the strong March wind, and yet your face is pale, and not glowing as I would expect. You are well, yes?'

Pauline's first reaction was that her personal well-being was no affair of his, but she was aware of a genuine concern behind the casual question.

'Of course I am, Dr Ghiberti. I'm just fine.' And then she actually heard herself saying, 'I've had two important pieces of news today.'

'Really, Sister? And were those pieces of news good?'

With those two inscrutable dark pools focusing upon her, Pauline felt as if he was reading her innermost thoughts. She wasn't sure that she wanted him to know them, but for some reason she found it impossible to turn away.

'My mother's getting married to our GP,' she announced abruptly.

'Ah, I see. And your mother lives in Beltonshaw?' he asked quietly.

'Yes, she and I live together. My elder sister is married, so it won't affect her much. My father died six years ago, and Dr—our GP lost his wife last year.'

'And you have always worked here? A good arrangement for as long as it was convenient to both you and your mother,' he commented. 'And now maybe it is time for a change, yes?'

'I don't know, Dr Ghiberti. I applied for Sister Beddows' post on this ward when she retires—she's on holiday this week——' She broke off and shook her head in a helpless gesture.

'And do you think you will take over from this sister, then?' he enquired, his eyes still on her face.

'No, I won't. I was turned down flat at the interview this afternoon, as a matter of fact.'

There was silence for a few moments while she wondered why on earth she had told him that. She thanked heaven that he could not know about the chill of rejection that engulfed her spirits like a damp grey fog.

Or could he? To her horror the tears that had stayed put during the nightmare interview in Mrs Gresham's office, and later on hearing her mother's unexpected announcement, now treacherously welled up. She turned away and opened a wall cupboard used for storing textbooks and old copies of the *Midwives' Chronicle*, pretending to look for something while fervently wishing that Dr Ghiberti would make a tactful exit and go back to his surgical wards.

She did not hear him rise from his chair, so she gasped when she felt his hands upon her shoulders. Unaccountably her knees turned to jelly, and her intake of breath ended on a sob. What a disaster, she thought, to let herself down in front of this man who reminded her of Giorgio. Yet, when the grip on her shoulders tightened, she had the most ridiculous longing to lean her head back against the broad chest behind her.

'I'm sorry, Dr—er——' she choked as the tears spilled down her face.

'Niccolo,' he reminded her gently. 'Do not worry, *cara mia*, all of us have to face the changes that come along in our lives, and it is not always easy to adjust. You are young, keen, and enthusiastic about your job—as I know to my cost!' He gave a teasing laugh, and in spite of her tears she smiled. 'Things will work out for you in a way you cannot now see. Take my word for it, Pauline.'

Still she could not speak, and she tried to take a deep breath to steady herself. His hands still rested on her in a warm and protective hold, and, although her back was towards him, she caught the tang of his aftershave—a spicy fragrance that blended with the heady masculinity that surrounded him like an aura, and of which she had been aware at their very first meeting. Was it only that morning at Joanna's bedside? It seemed so much longer.

Joanna! The thought of her patient hauled Pauline's thoughts back to her immediate duties. The six o'clock dose of ampicillin and flagyl was still in the treatment-room.

'Thank you—er, Niccolo,' she muttered, quickly wiping her eyes on the back of her hand. 'Excuse me now, please. I have to give Mrs Sandrini's medication.'

'Of course. She needs you, Sister Pauline.'

He removed his hands from her shoulders, and she dashed out of the office to retrieve the syringe in its plastic dish from the treatment-room.

When she returned he had gone, but a box of tissues had mysteriously appeared beside the injection tray.

Five days had passed since Joanna Sandrini had been successfully treated for an incipient paralytic ileus. Her course of antibiotics was completed, and she was taking a light diet. After evening visiting her brother and sister-in-law came to the office to ask how much longer she would have to stay in hospital.

'She'll probably be ready for discharge after the weekend,' Pauline told them. 'She'll have to take things very easily for a time.'

'We'll take good care of her, Sister,' said Joanna's brother. 'She'll have nothing to do but look after the baby. Of course, she's longing to see her husband, but he's been in Tokyo for some time now—working hard to bring off an important deal that will put his business back on a firm basis. They've had one hell of a worrying time this year,' he added in a lowered tone.

'Yes, Joanna had got very depressed because of Stefano being away for so long. That's why my husband asked her over to stay with us,' said the sister-in-law. 'And then all this happened!'

'I can see it's been a worrying time,' Pauline agreed. 'Joanna's lucky to have you both.'

'But she's fretting for Stefano, and wants to go back to Italy as soon as he returns from Tokyo,' said the sister-in-law. 'How soon will she and Toni be able to fly to Pisa?'

'I'd say about a month from the operation—but it depends on how she is. If somebody could accompany her——' began Pauline.

The woman's face fell. 'I'm afraid there's nobody. I've got my three young children, and my husband can't take time off work. I suppose we could get a private nurse from an agency, but then there'd be her air fare to pay as well as the fee. I'll enquire anyway—and thank you again for all you've done, Sister. We didn't know whether to send for Stefano or not, because their future could depend on his success with this deal. Apparently he's got it more or less in hand now, but there are details to be settled. It couldn't have happened at a worse time!'

When Pauline arrived home that evening, her mother handed her an airmail letter.

'Oh, great, it's from Jenny! I've been thinking a lot about her lately,' exclaimed Pauline, slitting open the envelope and eagerly scanning through the contents.

'How are the Alberis these days?' asked Helen.

'She says they're fine—and guess what? They're having a baby in September!'

'Oh, my! She won't be able to do so much to help Riccardo, then.'

Pauline frowned slightly. 'She says they're finding it difficult to get the right sort of trained staff, willing to live in and spend quite long periods on call. It seems they have a fair number of acute surgical cases, and need a theatre sister to cover for the summer.'

She looked across at her mother, with a sudden gleam in her blue-grey eyes and a questioning expression.

'You know, Mum, this could be just what I need. A completely fresh start, a whole new lifestyle, even speaking a different language—think of the challenge it would be!'

Helen looked doubtful. 'Don't rush into any sudden decisions, Pauline, and for heaven's sake don't think that you've got to go to Italy just because Graham and I——'

'No, Mum, it's not just that,' Pauline tried to explain. 'I've reached a crossroads in both my life and career, and I need a complete change—and I'd *love* to see Italy again, and Jenny!'

'Do consider it carefully, dear,' begged her mother, but Pauline's thoughts were flying on ahead in a rush of eager enthusiasm.

'I'll write to Jenny by tomorrow's post—no, better still, I'll telephone tonight! What's the time? Nine-fifteen—it'll be ten-fifteen there. And oh, *Mum*! I've just thought of something else—it'll be *Pisa* airport, and that's where Joanna Sandrini's going! *I* could accompany her and the baby, couldn't I? Hooray! What brilliant timing!'

And, to Helen's complete and utter bewilderment, Pauline twirled around the room on one foot, seized her mother in a bear-hug and then skipped out into the hall and lifted up the phone.

Pauline had a fortnight's holiday owing to her, and this was deducted from the month's notice she had to give to the health authority, leaving her only two weeks to work. These passed in a whirl of preparation; Joanna and her relations accepted her offer thankfully, and the flight was arranged for a Monday in the third week of April.

After the short domestic flight to Gatwick from Manchester they would fly on to Pisa and from there would travel by taxi to Florence, where rooms were booked at the Albergo Roccia Bianca, and where Stefano Sandrini would arrive to collect his wife and son to take them to their home at Vernio among the Tuscan hills. Pauline would then make the short journey to Fiesole and take up her appointment at the Clinico Silverio at the beginning of May.

Everything had changed in such a short time, and Pauline's depression melted away in the excitement of the coming adventure. Only one thing caused her a little sigh of regret at leaving Beltonshaw: she would see no more of the fascinating Niccolo Ghiberti. What a strange coincidence that she should be going to work in his part of the world at the same time that he was working in hers.

Not such brilliant timing, she had to admit. . .

CHAPTER TWO

PAULINE did not take long to discover that accompanying an anxious new mother and a fretful baby on two air flights was no easy assignment. From the moment when Joanna, Toni and all their luggage joined her taxi from Beltonshaw to Manchester Ringway Airport, she was fully occupied attending to their needs.

Joanna clung to her and said that she found Toni very heavy to carry, so Pauline asked for a wheelchair for her at the airport while she herself checked them in, obtained boarding cards, and sorted out the hand-luggage that would be needed on the flight. By the time they had reached Gatwick and been transferred eventually into the cabin of the Boeing 737, Pauline felt that she was earning every penny of her escort fee.

Three seats had been reserved, and she settled Joanna next to the window with the morning news-paper and a couple of magazines. She herself took the seat nearest the gangway, leaving the centre seat for Toni's carry-cot and the huge canvas holdall containing his disposable nappies, hand-towels, cotton wool wipes, baby cream and powder, waste-bag and a change of clothing. It was amazing how much para-phernalia such a tiny traveller needed.

Pauline had kept her own requirements to a mini-mum, but even so her capacious tapestry bag bulged with everything that might possibly be wanted on the journey. She wore a blue T-shirt with comfortable deep blue corduroy trousers and a matching jacket. Flat-heeled plain leather shoes completed the outfit she had chosen for practicality rather than style, and her newly washed hair was swept up into a topknot and secured with a ring of elasticated blue ribbon.

From the very start of their flight to Gatwick Toni had been wakeful and unhappy in the unfamiliar surroundings, and now Pauline took him on her lap before take-off.

'Come to Auntie Pauline, young man, and let Mummy have forty winks,' she told the wide-awake baby, but he continued to wriggle and make discontented noises, and when the engines revved up for the zoom along the runway he opened his mouth in an ear-splitting yell. With her own seat belt in position over the baby's special one, Pauline clasped her arms around him and whispered soothing sounds as she stroked his wagging head with her forefinger and softly put her lips to his flushed cheek. She tried gently patting his back.

'Shh-Shh, Toni, my love, there's a good boy,' she murmured over and over again, but the baby went on whimpering, flailing his little limbs in protest. When the seatbelts were unfastened Pauline laid him on a towel spread over her lap to check his nappy. She saw Joanna frown and put a hand to her forehead.

'Are you all right, Jo?' she asked quickly.

'I'm sorry, Pauline, but I've got a simply dreadful headache. I didn't sleep much last night, and I think Toni's picked up my tension. I don't care much for flying,' confessed Joanna apologetically.

Pauline noted the dark rings under her eyes, and silently thanked her lucky stars that this flight would only last three hours. She extracted a bottle of paracetamol tablets from her bag, and called to the stewardess to bring a glass of water.

Giving Joanna a boiled sweet to take the taste away, she prayed that Toni would settle, but as the Boeing droned high above northern France it became apparent that nothing was going to quieten him but a breast-feed. His yells were causing murmurs of disapproval among some of the other passengers, especially the man and woman seated behind them, and Pauline frowned at their lack of sympathy.

'They shouldn't be allowed to bring bawling brats on a scheduled flight,' grumbled a male voice nearby, and Pauline had to control herself to resist making a sharp retort.

At that moment the stewardess announced that their in-flight meal would be served, preceded by a drink of their choice from the portable bar which now appeared, propelled by the steward. Pauline realised that such a luxury would have to be foregone as far as she and Joanna were concerned

'Jo, dear, Toni's changed and ready for you, so let's give him his dinner,' she said gently, moving to the centre seat and helping Joanna to unbutton her blouse and unhook the front fastening of her bra.

'Here are your trays, madam,' announced the stewardess, but Pauline shook her head and waved them away.

'Mrs Sandrini is just about to feed her baby,' she explained. 'Would it be possible to save her meal and mine? And could you bring another glass of water for her?'

'Very well, madam,' replied the stewardess, thankful that no further assistance was required from her at a busy time.

Joanna was full of apologies for the inconvenience.
'I fed him just before we left, Pauline, so I really
don't know why he's carrying on like this.'

'Shh, Jo, don't worry so. I expect he wants the comfort of snuggling up to you. I'm no substitute for his
nice, soft, warm Mummy!' Pauline said with a smile.
'He'll settle once he's had a little suck, won't you,
Toni? Come on, let's get at your dinner!'

But Toni was in a very contrary mood, and while
all around them the other passengers were beginning
their meal Pauline found it quite a struggle to get the
cross little baby fixed in the correct position. He
kicked, waggled his head and howled in frustration as
Pauline twisted round in her seat, her fingers keeping
his mouth in contact with the nipple. All of a sudden
he latched on with a sharp tug, and Joanna could not
suppress an involuntary 'Ouch!'

The couple behind them began to make pointed
remarks that were clearly meant to be heard.

'Oh, this is too much! Talk about a bloody panto-
mime—just when we're trying to eat our food!'
grumbled the man. 'I'm going to have something to
say to the airline about this carry-on. Women ought
to use the toilets for this kind of thing.'

Although the majority of the passengers around
them were tolerant, and kindly disposed towards the
mother and baby, they had no wish to get involved in
an embarrassing scene by speaking up against the
strongly vocal couple. Instead they continued to eat
their meals in a rather awkward silence—and in a
typically English manner, thought Pauline irritably,
seeing Joanna's distress reflected in her flushed face.

'Anybody with any common sense would have
fed the child before the flight,' added the woman in a

sour tone. 'It shows no consideration whatever for other people, trapped in a situation they can't get away from.'

It was too much for Joanna. Her drawn features crumpled and tears began to trickle down her cheeks.

Pauline's eyes blazed, and her face flushed with anger. She was strongly tempted to raise her voice and declare her disgust at the insensitivity that these remarks showed, but she remembered her position as a midwife first and foremost, and the dignity required of her profession. To indulge in a shouting match with strangers would reduce her behaviour to their level, and besides, it was necessary to stay calm for the sake of the important work on which she was now engaged; assisting a mother to breast-feed her child. She drew several deep breaths to relax her tension, and spoke to Joanna in a clear, matter-of-fact tone.

'Don't cry, Jo, dear, just think about your baby. He's *much* more important than ignorant comments from those who don't know any better. He's feeding nicely now, so settle yourself and dry your eyes—here, use these tissues.'

The man behind them who had first complained now raised his voice angrily. 'I beg your pardon, madam! I heard that! Would you mind repeating what you said just now about the other long-suffering passengers?'

Pauline gritted her teeth and remained silent.

'Excuse me, madam! I asked you to repeat that offensive remark,' demanded the man again in a bully-ing tone, and Pauline could not make up her mind whether to reply or to maintain a dignified silence.

The problem was solved for her in a totally unexpec-ted way. A towering figure suddenly loomed above the seats and a deep, accented voice spoke with an

unmistakable authority that caused Pauline's heart to
do a somersault.

'Will somebody please explain what is the trouble
here? There is a mother feeding her baby with the only
food available to him, yes? Where is the problem?'

Pauline thought she must be dreaming. This was
impossible! Niccolo Ghiberti was working in
Beltonshaw on a year's exchange scheme, so how could
he be here on this flight to Pisa?

Joanna Sandrini had no such doubts.

'Oh, Pauline, look, it's Dr Ghiberti—that wonderful
doctor who came to my rescue when I was so ill. Oh,
thank God!' And she gave way to sobs of relief.

And there he was, standing right beside their three
seats, smiling down at them as Pauline tried to register
the incredible fact of his presence, just when they
needed him.

He leaned across her and spoke softly to Joanna.

'Hush, Signora Sandrini, it is important that you do
not upset yourself while you are feeding your little
one, no?'

Joanna smiled gratefully into the dark eyes that so
warmly reassured her, and as Toni was now feeding
contentedly she took the weight of his body on her
lap, leaving Pauline free to turn round in her seat and
find her voice.

'I—we had no idea that *you* were on the flight, Dr
Ghiberti. I didn't see you at Gatwick.'

'I don't think that you saw anything at the airport,
Sister Pauline, you were so taken up with your
charges,' he replied in a friendly way. 'I saw you in
the departure lounge, but you had no eyes for anybody
but Joanna and the baby and all the travel documents!
But it is good to see that you have found a new occupa-

tion with Mrs Sandrini. Things are working out for you after all!'

'Yes, we're going to Florence to meet her husband—but what are *you* doing?' she asked him. 'I thought you were under contract for a year.'

His smile vanished, and his face seemed to close up. 'So I am, but there is a matter which needs my attention, and I hope it will not take too long.'

He shrugged, clearly unwilling to discuss it, and Pauline turned back to Joanna, assisting her to change the baby over to the other breast halfway through the feed. She patted his back until he gave his usual satisfying burp, and the two young women exchanged a smile. Pauline tried not to look smug now that the complainers behind them had been shamed into silence by this imposing figure, who had stationed himself in the middle of the gangway beside them like a guard on sentry duty.

And there he remained, serenely matter-of-fact and apparently unconcerned, until Toni had finished feeding, then he leaned towards Pauline, lowering his voice.

'As soon as you ladies are ready for your meal, I will ask the stewardess to bring it to you, OK?'

'Thank you, Dr Ghiberti, you're an angel,' breathed Joanna, while it occurred to Pauline that he had probably only just started his own meal when he had come to their rescue. She took the baby in her arms while Joanna attended to her bra.

'I'd better have a fresh couple of bra-pads to tuck into this,' she said to Pauline, who reached with one hand into the holdall, feeling around for the packet of pads.

'Here, Sister Pauline, give him to me while you see

to Mrs Sandrini,' ordered Niccolo, holding out his arms
and carefully taking the baby from her. He held Toni
up against his shoulder, murmuring to him in a confi-
dential man-to-man way.

'Come, *piccolo bambino*, we men enjoy our food,
yes? And we know how to make a big *rutto* afterwards,
yes? Better than these females, no?'

Toni must have agreed with him, because he not
only gave a huge, windy burp, but also regurgitated a
long milky trail across the shoulder of the doctor's light
grey jacket and extending down to the well-cut lapel.

Joanna was buttoning her blouse-front, and did not
see, but Pauline looked up just as Niccolo held Toni
away from him to inspect the dribbled mess, and the
couple seated behind them nudged each other with
undisguised satisfaction at the calamity.

'Oh, my *God*,' gasped Pauline in horror.

Niccolo stared at Toni, and Toni stared right back
at Niccolo. The baby's round eyes were sweetly innocent, but the expression that lifted the corners of his
rosy mouth could only be described as a smirk.

It was too much for Pauline after the tension that
had surrounded the feed. She put up a hand to her
mouth, to hide the twitch she could not suppress, and
as Niccolo and Toni continued to confront each other
eye to eye her self-control gave way altogether. She
almost choked in her effort to stifle the laughter that
rose in her throat, but had no hope of succeeding, and
finally collapsed in her seat, shoulders shaking and
tears of mirth running down her face.

Joanna saw what had happened, and was overcome
with apologies.

'Pauline, how *can* you, after all that Dr Ghiberti
has done for us?' she cried. 'I'm so terribly sorry,

Doctor—here, take this towel and wipe it off. Oh, how simply awful! I'll pay for your jacket to be cleaned.'

Making a big effort to control herself, Pauline took the baby from Niccolo and tried to add her apologies.

'I—I'm sorry, Dr Ghiberti, I really am. It was your face—and Toni's—it was too funny!'

Try as she might, she could not keep a straight face, and Niccolo regarded her reproachfully as he mopped his lapel.

'So, this is my reward, then—and you have surprised me again, Sister Pauline. How was I to know that you would be so hysterical?'

She made another attempt to show regret for the ill-used jacket and her own heartless amusement, which made her as bad as the gloating couple behind them.

'I just don't know why I——' she began, then caught the twinkle in his dark eyes. For a moment they looked at each other blankly, and then both of them exploded with laughter, peal after peal, as if a baby being sick on a man's suit was the funniest thing in the world.

The other passengers exchanged glances and shrugs at the unaccountable behaviour of the strange couple; Toni gurgled happily as if sharing in the joke, and Pauline hugged him, not caring what anybody thought while those teasing eyes looked down into hers.

'You will excuse me now, ladies?' he said, when the stewardess brought their trays, and with a nod of approval he returned to his own seat at some distance from theirs.

With Toni asleep in his carry-cot, Pauline at last had an opportunity to look out of the windows on either side. A marvellous panorama was spread out under the blue dome of the April sky. A few scattered clouds

of trailing vapour were clearing below the throbbing
jet engines to reveal the glittering ultramarine of the
Mediterranean, dotted with rocky islands off its
northern shore.

The pilot's voice announced that the flight was on
time, the weather conditions good, and that they would
soon be in sight of the west coast of Italy. Pauline's
spirits rose; soon she would be in Florence, that most
beautiful and historic city, cradle of the Renaissance,
staying in a good hotel with all expenses paid. It was
an inviting prospect, and, even though she carried a
big responsibility for the mother and baby in her care,
there would surely be an opportunity to see some of
the famous views.

Her thoughts returned to Dr Ghiberti. What on
earth was he doing, returning to his homeland so
unexpectedly? He had given no reason, and had
seemed disinclined to talk about it—neither had he
returned to talk with her and Joanna since the incident
of the feed. Going back over what he had said, she
noted that although he had seen them at Gatwick he
had not approached them until they had needed his
assistance on the plane—which meant that if they had
not got into difficulties they would never have known
that he was on the flight.

His business must be something that he wanted to
keep to himself, and was nothing to do with her anyway. What an enigmatic man he was! And so
extraordinarily handsome—more so than Giorgio had
been, she now admitted. In fact, his resemblance to her
faithless Italian lover now seemed much less striking.
Giorgio belonged to the past, and she realised that she
had forgotten the pain he had caused her.

But that was no reason to start daydreaming about

Niccolo, and she made a conscious effort to dismiss him from her thoughts. A new adventure was about to begin, and as the flight neared its destination she looked down eagerly on a breathtaking Tuscan landscape of green and gold. Verdant pastureland gave way to the greyish-green of olive groves, with clusters of straight, dark-leaved cypresses and sun-baked red roofs. Pauline's thoughts began to drift, but she pulled herself up sharply and straightened her back. It was time to start preparing Joanna and Toni for the landing.

When the Boeing touched down at Pisa's Galileo Galilei Airport, Pauline needed all her wits about her to shepherd the mother and baby through Passport Control and Customs, and pick up their luggage from the carousel. There was the additional necessity of speaking Italian, but she managed to make herself understood using simple phrases.

Out of the corner of her eye she caught sight of Dr Ghiberti wheeling a luggage trolley; he appeared to be hesitating, as if wondering whether to approach them. When Joanna saw him and waved he came to a decision, and turned in their direction.

'Are you being met, Pauline?'

'No, we have to take a taxi to Florence—Firenze,' she added, thinking the Italian name now more appropriate.

'Ah, I go there also, but by train. I may perhaps call a taxi for you, yes?'

'Thank you very much, Niccolo,' she replied gratefully, truly relieved to have some help. Her duties were beginning to weigh quite heavily on her shoulders, and now that she was in a foreign country, with two other people totally dependent on her and a whole pile of

luggage to be transported, she felt a twinge of anxiety
that she knew she must hide.

Within seconds he had heaved their luggage on to
his own trolley and wheeled it towards the exit, while
Pauline carried Toni in his cot, and Joanna trudged
wearily beside her. Brilliant sunshine greeted them as
they emerged from Arrivi Internazionali and Niccolo
gestured to the driver of the nearest yellow taxi-cab.
Pauline handed Joanna and the baby into the back seat
while the doctor helped the driver to stow their luggage
in the boot. She held out her hand to him just before
she got in.

'*Molte grazie*, Dottore Niccolo!'

'*Prego!* Take care, Sister Pauline!'

She thought she saw a flicker of concern in the
eyes that returned her heartfelt look. Had he held her
hand for just a fraction of a second longer than was
necessary? She must have shown some of her apprehension in her face, for he frowned slightly, his
dark brows lowering above his lofty nose. Under the
bright sky of his homeland his skin appeared a clear
olive, his brows sable-black. *Definitely* superior to
Giorgio.

'What address shall I give to the driver?' he asked.

'Albergo Roccia Bianca, *per favore*,' she said
smartly, to show that she was able to cope with direc-
tions, and noted that the expressive eyebrows lifted a
little. As the driver nodded and started the engine,
Pauline turned and waved.

'*Buongiorno*, Niccolo!'

'*Buongiorno, signora e signorina e bambino!*' he
called after them, and turned away. Pauline pictured
him going to board his train, and speculated about his
destination in Florence, and why he had so suddenly

left Beltonshaw General. Surely not because of any trouble in the Department of Surgery? Then why should he be so cagey about it?

There was little time to ponder over Niccolo Ghiberti's affairs as their taxi sped along the *auto-strada*. Joanna leaned back in her seat with her eyes closed, her tightly set mouth and fidgeting fingers betraying her inner tension. Pauline clasped the still sleeping Toni and looked grave. It was high time that Joanna shook off the 'baby blues' common to most new mothers in the first week or two—even taking into account the unpleasant complications she had experienced. Pauline pinned her hopes on the reunion with Stefano, expected in Florence during the next twenty-four hours or so.

She scarcely saw the outskirts of the city, crowded and noisy with traffic hurtling along on what was to her the wrong side of the road. When they entered the old city they were in a restricted zone, where only authorised access vehicles were permitted, and in a few minutes more they drew up outside a tall, narrow-fronted building in a cobbled street where the houses seemed to lean towards their opposite numbers on the other side, and balconies jutted out for four storeys. The quaintly carved stone niches in the walls and the shuttered windows would have fascinated Pauline if she had not had to give all her attention to her charges.

The driver unloaded the luggage and carried it up a few worn stone steps and into a dimly lit hallway.

'*Benvenute, signora e signorina!*' cried a handsome, well-built woman in a black dress, coming towards them smiling and holding out her arms in welcome. She introduced herself as the proprietress and said that she knew Signora Sandrini, Stefano's mother. She sighed delightedly over *il bambino bello*, and ushered them into a lift that whisked them up to the third floor and a pleasant apartment consisting of a living-room and one large and one small bedroom, with balconies that overlooked the jumbled roofs of the city and afforded a glimpse of the Arno flowing through its heart.

A little carved wooden cradle was ready to receive the baby, and flowers and fruit had arrived with a card from Stefano. A neat little buggy had also been delivered, much to Pauline's satisfaction, for it meant that Toni could be taken out for rides in the fresh air—an exercise that would also benefit his mother and give them all an opportunity to see a little of Florence.

The proprietress explained that there had been a telephone call from a business partner of Signor Sandrini, to say that Stefano would be flying from Tokyo to Milan on the following day, and taking the train to Florence on the Wednesday. Joanna's reaction to this news was disappointing.

'Whatever will he think of me, Pauline? I look such a mess! God knows how I'd have coped without you today—how will I manage Toni when you've gone to that clinic? Not to mention everything else!'

There was a note of real panic in her voice that seriously worried Pauline. She realised that Joanna was depressed, and also that she herself had little or no experience in dealing with mothers after their discharge from the postnatal ward. She was not sure how to manage a possible case of clinical postnatal depression, but encouraged Joanna to rest and revitalise herself in preparation for the reunion with her husband in two days' time.

'Everything will be so much easier when Stefano's with you again, Jo. And I'm sure that his mother will be understanding when she comes to look after you and Toni at Vernio. You'll be fine, love, I know you will!' she assured the anxious Joanna, whose eyes were hollow with fatigue and whose mouth drooped at the very thought of her mother-in-law's ministrations.

'Do you *have* to go to this clinic, Pauline?' she asked, and Pauline also began to wonder what she should do. Jenny and Riccardo were expecting her this week.

A plump maid arrived with a tray of tea, mineral water and a jug of milk. As soon as they had refreshed themselves, Pauline insisted that Joanna went straight to bed.

'Don't worry, love. I'm here to look after Toni,' she said firmly.

'But you won't see anything of Florence!'

'Florence can wait until it's convenient, Jo. As a matter of fact, I shall be quite glad of an early night myself,' smiled Pauline, thankful that they had arrived without any worse mishap than the scene on the plane. Her eyes softened momentarily at the memory of Niccolo's timely appearance, and she allowed herself to imagine a chance meeting in Florence at some point. . .

A peremptory squeak from a newly awakened Toni banished such unlikely daydreams from her mind.

Stefano turned out to be a good ten years older than Joanna, and shorter and stouter than Pauline had imagined. Though he looked the part of a bustling businessman with important matters on his mind, she was in no doubt about his genuine regret for his long absence and apparent neglect of his wife and baby son.

'*O mia Giovanna, cara mia! Mi perdoni per la mia assenza*?'

His passionate plea for forgiveness was unmistakably sincere, and Pauline tactfully withdrew from the lounge, where the couple were locked in a tearful embrace, as soon as he arrived.

Very soon, however, Joanna called to her and introduced her to Stefano, who seized both of her hands in his and kissed them to show his gratitude for all her kindness to his wife. Joanna endlessly sang her praises as a midwife and baby-nurse, and Stefano lost no time in asking if she would accompany them to Vernio, to continue her care of the mother and baby.

She regretfully declined, as she was due to take up her duties at the Clinico Silverio at the weekend, but a compromise was reached, with Pauline agreeing to stay with them at the Albergo Roccia Bianca until Saturday, allowing Joanna a further three days of expert help from the midwife on whom she had come to rely so much. *Too* much, Pauline decided, telling herself that Joanna would bounce back to normality when she was settled at Vernio.

That Wednesday evening she asked the couple if it would be convenient for her to go out for an hour or two, and they immediately agreed that it was high time that she had some time off to relax.

'Yes, Pauline, you must go out for the *passeggiata*—the evening stroll that the Florentines enjoy. Walking out and meeting each other, to talk and exchange the news and gossip of the day, as they always have done from past times,' Stefano told her. He was sitting on the side of the armchair in which Joanna reclined, looking down at her with such tender concern that

Pauline's eyes misted over, and she hastily closed the door behind her.

All of a sudden she realised how tired she was. Joanna and Toni had kept her well occupied, and the nights had been broken by feeds in the small hours. Now at last she had a chance to see something of the city in which she had been tucked away for the past forty-eight hours, out of sight and earshot of the life going on all around her.

She took a long breath and looked at her watch. Six-thirty on a fine spring evening. She hoisted her leather bag over her shoulder and smoothed a hand down over her denim skirt. A plain navy jacket over a tailored white cotton blouse, teamed with comfortable but stylish navy shoes seemed suitable wear for the *passeggiata*. After descending in the lift to the ground floor passage, she went out into the narrow street and set out towards the *piazza*—the square that she remembered seeing on the day that the taxi had brought them from Pisa. Had that only been two days ago? It seemed an age. . .

CHAPTER THREE

THE evening was clear and warm, more like June than April, and the streets were thronging with townspeople mingling with tourists of many nationalities, including a fair number of Americans on the trail of European culture—some of them retired couples on a long-awaited tour.

Pauline was surprised to see whole Florentine families, from grandparents to children, strolling and greeting each other, stopping to watch a group of masked dancers in the *piazza* or taking a convivial drink at a pavement table. She was thrilled to be part of it all, and looked around in unconcealed delight.

Gradually it dawned on her that she herself was generating a fair amount of interest among the dark-eyed Florentine youths, whose heads turned in the direction of the pretty, unaccompanied blonde girl. They eyed her boldly up and down, and one or two asked hopefully, 'You speak English?'

She smiled, turning away her face and lowering her eyes while walking on as if she had a definite desti-nation in view; she remembered how she and Jenny had walked on air two years ago, when going to meet Riccardo and Giorgio in Rome and again in Venice. Their two admirers had followed them from one city to another, abandoning their own holiday plans just to be near the two English girls.

She jumped to one side with a little cry as a swarthy motor-scooterist in leather jacket and jeans leaned over close to her as his machine roared past. Doing a rapid U-turn, he came back to pass her again, stretching out at a dangerous angle to exclaim, '*Bellissima*!'

Such open and undisguised admiration from young and not-so-young males was a fairly unusual experience for Pauline, and although she averted her demure blue-grey eyes from their frank stares, she was not really offended; she would have been a strange girl if she had resented the fact that men found her desirable! Even so, she was disconcerted when the persistent scooterist swung round for the third time and brought his machine to a halt by her side.

The *piazza* was surrounded on two sides by a thick-walled building of weathered brown stone, with high, narrow windows dating from when it had been a fortress. Pauline found herself trapped in the corner where the two walls met, with no way of escaping her pursuer. When she tried to pass round him he smiled, barring her way and indicating the pillion saddle.

'I am Enrico. What are you called, please?'

'Er—no, I do not want——' began Pauline, all her Italian phrases either inappropriate or lost to memory in this embarrassing situation. 'Please, let me pass. I wish to walk!'

He smiled and nodded. 'OK, we walk, *signorina*, and I park the scooter, yes? You like coffee? Ice-cream? Good wine?' He held out his leather-clad arm and seized her shoulder, clearly under the impression that she had agreed to spend time in his company.

'No, no, let me go!' She stepped back and tried to shake off his hand. The scooter swayed to one side, and he only just managed to right it in time.

'*Signorina*, you no worry. You come with me and we go to——'

'*Basta*! That is enough!'

The sound of a deep and very angry voice behind Enrico broke in on the attempted pick-up, and had a very prompt effect on the young Casanova. Giving one glance up at the voice's owner, he restarted the scooter and shot forward, disappearing from the *piazza* and down a side-street.

'Young idiot! He'll kill himself on that contraption one of these days, and any silly girl who's sitting behind him.'

Pauline froze, clutching her shoulder-bag. She knew that voice. She looked down at the intricate paving on which stood a pair of feet—long, narrow, well-proportioned feet in thonged leather sandals, planted in front of her as if waiting for her to look up and see the body to which they belonged. As her eyes travelled up a pair of very long legs and came to rest on an open-necked shirt, showing an expanse of broad chest on which a silver cross hung, she knew without looking any higher that she would see the face of Niccolo Ghiberti. And, sure enough, there he was, his patrician features looking down on her with both pleasure and sternness.

She could think of nothing to say as her heart beat a tattoo against her ribs. Was this really a coincidence? Could he by any chance have been loitering in the vicinity of the Albergo Roccia Bianca? Or had she wished so hard for him to appear that in this magic city her wish had been granted? Oh, heavens, what *nonsense* I'm thinking, she rebuked herself.

'You should not be walking out alone, Pauline,' he was saying. Why on earth did she have to blush? She smiled and gave a shrug.

'It's still daylight, and there are hordes of people

about, Niccolo. It was my own fault for not making it
quite clear to him that——'

'I say again, it is not wise for an attractive young
girl to wander alone in any city at this hour,' he said
emphatically. 'As soon as you sit down, or stop to look
at a building, or a shop selling souvenirs, it will be
assumed that you are—er—available for dating.
Joanna should have warned you.'

How could she object to a word like attractive, even
though he made her feel like a naughty schoolgirl?

'I'll remember in future,' she replied rather lamely.
'Only—I may not get another chance to do this.'

He relented with a smile, and patted her shoulder
like a teacher approving a good pupil. '*Va bene*. And
now, as you are taking the *passeggiata* alone on such
a fine evening, may I offer to be your guide? I have
a couple of hours to spare if it would be convenient.'

This was unbelievable. Pauline smiled her accept-
ance, though warned herself not to appear too eager.

'How kind of you, Niccolo, I'd like that,' she said,
with what she hoped was the right degree of friendliness. 'This is the second time you've come to the rescue
this week!'

'Ah, yes, how is Mrs Sandrini? I thought she did
not look too well on the plane.'

'She's finding it hard to cope, and seems to have no
confidence in herself,' admitted Pauline, and went on
to explain that Signor Sandrini had arrived that day,
which was why she had some free time at last.

'You poor girl—you must be quite worn out! Shall
we sit down on this bench and I will fetch an ice-cream
from the *gelateria* over there? What flavour do you
prefer?'

'Oooh, have they got chocolate ones?' she asked,

thankful to sit down. Her knees had gone unaccountably weak for some reason. When he returned with huge double cones, containing generous scoops of both chocolate and coffee ice-cream, she soon realised why Italian ices were acclaimed as the best in the world.

He sat down beside her and together they happily demolished their delicious concoctions. Pauline felt like a child being given a treat, and gradually relaxed; it was impossible to be too formal while licking an enormous ice-cream cone! Her tiredness magically lifted, and she gazed around the *piazza* in complete fascination. Everything was so excitingly different here. . .

Including the man who sat beside her, stretching out his long legs in front of him. He really was quite devastatingly good-looking, with that combination of Latin colouring and finely chiselled features that gave him an aristocratic look, like a Roman senator in the time of the Caesars, she thought—no, more like a Medici, she corrected herself. A member of that great and powerful Florentine family of merchants and bankers who had infiltrated the royal families of Europe and even reached the papal throne. Yes, he was like a Medici—and appropriately, for the very word meant 'doctors'—a Florentine by birth and inheritance.

'What are your first impressions of Florence?' he asked.

'Beautiful—*bellissima*!' she breathed. 'The colours of the buildings in this evening light are simply out of this world.'

'Ah, you have noticed the colours of Florence? The light has a special quality here that is not found anywhere else, or so the artists say.'

'Is it the effect of all those centuries on the stone-work, which has turned them gold and brown and orangey-red?' mused Pauline, stealing a sideways look at his profile.

Surely their meeting had to be a coincidence—yet there was no mistaking his pleasure at being with her, and she secretly forgave the scooterist for his unwanted attentions which had led to such a happy consequence. Whatever would her colleagues at the Maternity Department say if they could see her now?

'Where are you staying, Niccolo?' she enquired casually.

There was the slightest hesitation before he replied, 'I've been offered a room at Santa Maria Nuova while I'm here.'

Pauline wondered if this was a church or monas-tery. There were so many Sans and Santas in Florence—even the railway terminus was called Santa Maria Novella.

Niccolo saw that she was none the wiser, and added, 'The hospital where I trained. And you, Pauline? Do you stay at the *albergo* with the Sandrinis?'

'Till Saturday,' She went on to tell him their plans to go to their home at Vernio, where Stefano's mother would look after his wife and baby. She also confided some of her fears about Joanna's mental state, and he turned down the corners of his mouth in sympathy.

'That is not good. We must hope that the old lady is patient, and understands that Joanna has been through much trauma. And, of course, with the additional problem of living in a foreign country with a foreign husband!'

'That can be a difficulty, though I have a nurse friend

who is very happily married to a—an Italian doctor,'
ventured Pauline, cursing her tendency to blush so
easily. 'It depends on the people, really, doesn't it?'

He pursed his lips thoughtfully. 'Pauline, would it
not be possible for you to stay with Joanna at Vernio
for a while, as she relies on you and trusts you?'

'Yes, Stefano has asked me,' she admitted. 'But I
am due to start work this weekend at a small hospital
near Fiesole—the Clinico Silverio—run by the the
friend I mentioned, and her husband.'

He turned and looked at her in surprise.

'Riccardo Alberi? He and I were in medical school
together.'

'You know them?' cried Pauline, her eyes wide.

'No, not these days—and I have not met your friend,
his wife. I do not care for that kind of private hospital
for wealthy hypochondriacs who can pay to be pam-
pered. And I cannot picture you at such a place,
Pauline.'

Her heart sank a little at his stated disapproval, and
she felt that she owed some loyalty to the Alberis.

'It's just a short contract while I sort out what I'm
going to do with my life,' she said lightly. 'Actually,
I'm quite looking forward to something completely different from Beltonshaw General. They need a theatre
sister to live in and be on call.'

He appeared unconvinced. 'You are such a superior
nurse and midwife, Pauline, worthy of better things.
You will soon be bored with the idle rich!'

Pauline had no intention of wasting a heaven-sent
evening in Niccolo's company by arguing over
the merits or otherwise of a hospital about which
she really knew very little; he could be right, for all
she knew.

'I decided to take up this job when I didn't get the postnatal ward at Beltonshaw—and my mother got engaged to Dr Stafford,' she added quickly. 'I need a complete change, and it's a chance to work with a very good friend again. And I love Italy!'

His face remained serious. 'It is not my business, of course, but I think you would be better staying with Joanna Sandrini.'

Pauline did not reply, but finished her ice-cream, discreetly wiping her mouth on the paper serviette supplied with the cone.

'How far is it to the Arno?' she asked.

He got up, tacitly agreeing to drop a subject on which they did not see eye to eye.

'All streets in Florence lead to the Arno! Come and walk with me along the Porta Santa Maria to the Ponte Vecchio.'

He offered his arm, and together they joined the strollers making their way up and down the ancient thoroughfare towards the old bridge that had linked the north and south banks of the Arno for nearly seven hundred years.

Its overhanging jewellery boutiques and goldsmiths' shops were now closed, but Niccolo drew Pauline into the centre of the bridge, beneath an elegant arched terrace, where they leaned upon the parapet and gazed downriver to where the graceful curves of the Ponte Santa Trinita were reflected in the darkening water.

The light was beginning to fade and the air was cooler. As she stood on the world-famous bridge Pauline's chief sensation was of the warmth of Niccolo's shoulder, lightly touching hers as he pointed to the spot on the Lungarno where it was said that Dante had first caught sight of the beautiful Beatrice, who was to become the love of his life and the inspiration for his *Divina Commedia*.

The old buildings along the Lungarno glowed with warm tints of russet and apricot, and in the distance the purple hills deepened to indigo, lit here and there by lamps and the glimmer of lighted windows. It was a scene which at this hour of dusk seemed not essentially changed since Dante had lived and loved and written his works of genius.

There was silence between them for a timeless moment, and Pauline hardly dared to breathe for fear of breaking the spell of this incredible dream that she was having of standing on the Ponte Vecchio with Niccolo Ghiberti. The other strollers receded from her consciousness, the sound of their voices faded away. . .

At last she drew a long, sighing breath, and her whole frame trembled slightly as it ended. Niccolo was immediately concerned.

'Pauline, you are getting cold. It is time that I offered you something to eat. There is a little *trattoria*——'

'Oh, no, I must get back to the *albergo*,' she said at once. 'Joanna and Stefano will be wondering where I've got to.'

'And maybe you are thinking about little Toni, yes?' His voice was soft and deep in her ear, as if he too were having to collect his thoughts together after some private journey of his own.

'Yes, I do think of Toni,' she murmured. 'Oh, Niccolo, I hope that everything will be all right for that little baby.'

With her arm tucked under his, they returned to the Porta Santa Maria, heading for the *piazza* and the narrow street leading back to the *albergo*. As they were about to turn into it there was a sudden noise of

approaching motorcycles, and several confused shouts
as two scooters roared out of the side-street, scattering
pedestrians out of their path. Pauline screamed and
jumped backwards, and immediately felt Niccolo's
arms around her as he angrily shouted a warning to
the two young riders, who appeared to be completely
out of control.

Everything happened so quickly. An elderly
American couple, standing with their backs to the
oncoming scooters, were deep in a heated argument
about which direction to take. One of the riders managed to swerve in time to avoid them, but the other
struck the stout old lady a glancing blow which caused
her to spin round and fall heavily. Her husband stag-
gered but regained his balance, and gazed in utter
horror at the figure of his wife sprawled on the flag-
stones, her head thrown back and her face blank and
lifeless. The scooterist, thrown off-balance by the
impact, let go of the steering and within seconds was
on the ground beneath his machine.

An uproar of shouts and accusations filled the air
as the old man ran to kneel at his wife's side. A New
England accent broke through his anguished sobs.

'My God, she's dead—my Sophy's dead, and that
young bastard's killed her! He's killed my wife—my
darling!'

Niccolo let go of Pauline and in two strides was
beside the the victim.

'*Mi scusi—sono un dottore*—er, please, let me
see her.'

The man was holding her right hand and kissing it
frantically. Niccolo took hold of her limp left hand and
searched for a pulse, then gently put his hand beneath
her blouse and felt for the heartbeat, at which he

nodded to her husband in reassurance. He pulled up each eyelid in turn, examining the pupils.

'Does she need the kiss of life?' whispered Pauline, prepared to assist.

'No, she's breathing—heart's a bit weak and thready. She must have hit the road with the back of her head and she has concussion.'

He took off his jacket to roll up and put under her head, and, raising his voice, he spoke in rapid Italian to the growing crowd of onlookers. Pauline made out the words '*telefono*', '*emergenza*' '*ambulanza*', and '*pronto, pronto!*' He then asked for a newspaper, and a man handed him that evening's copy of *Il Corriere della Sera*. Niccolo rolled it tightly and made it into a ring, which he placed firmly around the old lady's neck as a temporary spinal collar.

Pauline had an arm around the distraught husband's shoulders when she saw the woman's eyelids flutter.

'She's opening her eyes. Look, she's coming round!' she breathed, and the husband burst into another torrent of words.

'It's all right, Sophy, I'm right here, darling. Speak to me, Sophy, speak to your Frank!'

The old lady began to moan feebly, putting her right hand up to her face.

'I think there is no fracture of the long bones,' Niccolo muttered out of the corner of his mouth to Pauline. 'Though she could have cracked her pelvis or——'

At that moment Pauline felt a tap on her shoulder from a woman who told her that the motor-scooterist was badly hurt and losing blood. She got up and hurried the few yards to where the young man lay groaning on the ground. His ashen-faced companion, assisted

by bystanders, had lifted the scooter off his body, to
reveal his face covered in blood from a deep gash
across the cheek. Pauline at once saw that his left leg
was twisted and lying in an unnatural position, and
that a large, dark bloodstain was spreading rapidly over
the lower leg of his jeans.

She swallowed, trying to think clearly about pri-
orities as she knelt beside him. The signs pointed to
a fracture of the shin-bone with associated haemorrhage, in which case his condition was serious, and
something had to be done at once to bring the bleeding
under control. Turning to the woman who had summoned her, Pauline told her to ask the doctor to come.
This led to furious protests from Frank.

'Let that young jerk wait, Doc! My wife needs you,
goddammit!'

Niccolo rolled his eyes at the dilemma, and frowned
as he came to Pauline's side. 'How is he?' he asked
abruptly.

'I'm pretty sure he's got a fractured tibia and it must
have pierced the surface,' she told him quickly. 'You
can see that he's losing a fair bit of blood. What about
a tourniquet?'

'Yes, below the knee, and *now*,' the doctor replied
urgently. 'Have we a belt—scarf—a length of cord?
Anything to tie round the leg?'

The other scooterist produced a leather belt, but
Niccolo rejected it as too rigid. A silk scarf offered by
a woman was too flimsy. Pauline drew out the linen
belt threaded through the loops at the waist of her
denim skirt.

'What about this? It's strong but quite pliable. And
should we try to cut the leg of his jeans if we can get
some scissors from somewhere?'

'No, no, do not move the limb, Pauline,' answered Niccolo, taking the belt and tying it twice round the youth's leg just below the knee. Having tied a reef-knot, he took a pencil from his pocket.

'This may be a little uncomfortable,' he told the young man in Italian, sliding the pencil under the knot and twisting it round to tighten the constriction. The injured man groaned, and Pauline wiped his face gently with a handkerchief taken from her bag.

'*La bella signorina inglese*,' he moaned faintly, and Pauline gasped in recognition of her admirer Enrico, who had tried to lure her away on his scooter earlier that evening. She carefully laid the folded handkerchief over the jagged laceration that extended from the side of his nose to the left jaw.

'Don't worry, Enrico,' she said quietly in Italian. 'Your eye is unharmed; that is the most important thing.'

A police car drew up, and two officers took some details. Frank and Sophy Partridge were from Massachusetts and on a first trip to Europe; Frank left the police in no doubt of his views.

'Damned motorcycles ought to be banned in a place like this! Nothing but a menace! Don't let me near that hooligan, or I'll throttle him!'

Ignoring the disturbance, Niccolo put Pauline in charge of Enrico, with instructions for the care of the tourniquet.

'Hold the pencil, Pauline, and release it every three minutes by your wristwatch to let the circulation flow through,' he ordered. 'I had better stay with the old lady if you're happy about this—OK?'

Pauline nodded, and he gave her a quick thumbs-up sign of approval.

When an olive-green van drew up and two black-hooded figures jumped out, Pauline thought for one bewildered moment that they were members of some mysterious organisation, come to take the law into their own hands, but when she heard them greet Niccolo by name and produce stretchers and blankets, she realised that this was the ambulance service. Were they a special order of monks? she wondered.

'My Sophy's not gonna travel in the same conveyance as that young fool—no way!' Frank declared with finality, and no amount of reasoning or pleading would budge him.

A quick consultation took place between Niccolo and the two attendants.

'There is another ambulance ready to leave, Doctor,' said one of them. 'It is but a matter of minutes from the Piazza del Duomo. If your nurse and I stay with the injured man, my driver will take you and the old lady and her husband to Santa Maria Nuova.'

Pauline urged Niccolo to agree to this suggestion, and with a last anxious look at her he got into the van with the Partridges.

Somebody had managed to get a message to Enrico's mother, who arrived just as the second ambulance drew up. While Pauline felt sorry for the tearful, over-weight woman, who sobbed and called upon the Blessed Virgin to aid her injured son, it seemed reasonable to point out that nobody had been killed, and that the accident could have been very much worse.

Getting into the van with the mother and son, she had to hold up her beltless skirt which, like her blouse and jacket, was smeared with Enrico's blood and dirt from the paving; sitting beside him and constantly monitoring the tourniquet, she tried to give him what comfort and reassurance she could.

The van took only a few minutes to arrive at the imposing collonaded front entrance of the Ospedale Santa Maria Nuova, which seemed more like a palace than a hospital to Pauline. Its lighted windows glowed in the deepening dusk, and the Italian flag fluttered above the main entrance, its red, white and green colours no longer distinguishable.

The ambulance went to the left of the main building towards an illuminated sign, 'Pronto Soccorso' surmounted by a red cross indicating that it was the First Aid Department for accidents and emergencies. White-uniformed orderlies hurried forward with a stretcher trolley on to which Enrico was carefully transferred and then wheeled up a wide corridor to a curtained cubicle for examination and a preliminary clean-up.

Pauline sat with his mother in the waiting area, feeling oddly at home with her surroundings, almost enjoying the atmosphere of a great hospital; the very smell of the place seemed comfortingly familiar. She knew that she would be expected back at the *albergo*, but Enrico's mother clung to her and begged her to stay to hear the verdict on her son. Pauline looked around for a telephone, but there seemed nobody free to attend to her.

Mrs Partridge's X-rays, still wet and hanging on metal frames, were brought from Radiologia by Niccolo, who was obviously on home ground here, an authoritative and respected figure. He told her that they revealed a dislocated left shoulder joint but no fracture of the skull or other bones.

'She is well-covered, like a cushion, yes?' he remarked to Pauline with a smile, and translated the casualty officer's comments to Frank when he accom-

panied his wife back from X-Ray. She was to be
admitted for a reduction of the shoulder joint under
a general anaesthetic, and, in view of her age and the
mild concussion she had austained, a period
of forty-eight hours of rest and observation was
recommended.

'Tell him she's to have a private room and the best
service they can deliver,' Frank ordered, and Pauline
nodded to the nurse who was admitting the old lady.

'*Camera privata, per favore.*'

Sophy Partridge, now fully conscious, had begun to
argue with her husband, and Pauline felt that this was
a good sign. Frank turned to say goodbye to Niccolo
before going with her to her waiting hospital bed.

'You took good care of her, Doc, and I want to tell
you I appreciate it. But, so help me, I'm gonna sue
that guy who nearly did for her.'

'I think he is going to pay in other ways for his
reckless driving, Mr Partridge,' said Niccolo gravely.
'He will have a leg in plaster and go on crutches for
many weeks. And for his life there will be a scar on
his face to remind him of this day.'

The old man stumped off, muttering threats under
his breath, and Niccolo raised his expressive black eyebrows at Pauline, who smiled and shrugged.

The casualty officer then beckoned to them both,
and asked them to come into the cubicle where Enrico
lay. Pauline suppressed a gasp of dismay at the sight
of the bone protruding through the skin of the lower
limb, proving that her initial diagnosis had been all
too accurate.

The doctor commended them both for their first
aid care.

'The tibia and fibula are fractured, and the tibial

shaft is visible, as you see. You did well to put on the tourniquet. We shall take X-rays and I think he will need a Steinman pin through each fragment. We shall admit him for operation tonight, and plaster with traction afterwards.'

'And his face?' asked Pauline, giving Enrico a smile, though his eyes were closed.

'It will need suturing at the same time,' replied the doctor. 'As with Mrs Partridge, we have given a tetanus injection and also pain relief. He is looking better now, and the bleeding has stopped, thanks to you both. Can you explain these details to his mother, Ghiberti?'

It was a relief when Enrico's father arrived, recalled from his evening shift on the railways. He and his wife accompanied their son to X-Ray and then to a male surgical ward to be prepared for orthopaedic surgery. By now his face was so swollen and bruised as to be unrecognisable, and Pauline sincerely pitied him when she whispered goodnight and good luck.

'I simply *must* go now, Niccolo,' she apologised, indicating the clock on the wall, which showed nearly half-past nine.

'You must not walk back, Pauline. I will call a taxi for you,' he said firmly. '*O mio Dio*! This is not a good end to the evening, no?'

'Not your fault,' she replied with a grin. 'And I've been introduced to your hospital!'

His dark eyes rested on her with a softness in their depths that turned her knees to water, but she suddenly realised what a sight she must appear.

'Niccolo, could I telephone the Albergo Roccia Bianca to let the Sandrinis know what's happened?' she asked, and he was at once concerned and apologetic. When the call had been made and a taxi ordered, he showed her to a ladies' cloakroom, where she washed and tidied herself a little, adjusting her unbelted skirt with a safety-pin given to her by one of the nurses on duty. When she emerged, Niccolo walked with her to the entrance to await her taxi.

'Tell me, Niccolo, who are those hooded ambulancemen? Do they belong to a religious order?'

He laughed. 'Perhaps some of them do! They come from all walks of life, and are pledged to give at least an hour a week, freely, to provide a service for the people of Florence. The Brotherhood of Mercy must be the oldest first aid institution in the world, and is unique to this city.'

Pauline heard the note of pride in his voice as he went on to explain that the Brotherhood, founded over six hundred years ago, worked in shifts around the clock from their headquarters in the cathedral square.

'Whether it is to bring a sick child into hospital, or to comfort a dying old woman, you can see them dashing out at any time of the day or night,' he told her. 'They give more than just first aid care.'

'And why do they wear those hoods?' she enquired.

'To hide their identity.' He smiled. 'Not everyone wants to be recognised, no? As I told you, Paolina, they come from all walks of life!'

Paolina. How charming it sounded on his lips, this Italian version of her name. Before she could ask more about the amazing Brotherhood, the taxi drew up and he helped her into it. They scarcely had time to say goodnight before the driver zoomed away.

When she reached the *albergo* she dashed up to the Sandrinis' apartment, half expecting them to be annoyed at her long absence, or at least reproachful, but she was greeted with nothing but relief. It seemed that they had had a difficult evening with Toni, and Joanna was tired and tearful. Pauline at once adjusted her mood and manner to the familiar task of initiating Joanna into the joys of motherhood.

When Toni had been tucked into his cot and the Sandrinis' bedroom door was shut, Pauline took a welcome shower and got ready for bed. Before going to it she opened the door on to her little balcony and stepped outside. She was restless, her mind a kaleidoscope of conflicting emotions. As the soft, cool breeze ruffled her hair and soothed her flushed cheeks she reflected upon how different her life had become during the past three days. Beltonshaw was another world that had nothing to do with the present.

There was a sudden tap at her bedroom door, and at once she returned to the room.

'Yes? *Avanti*!' she called, fully expecting Joanna to enter with some new problem; she smiled in readiness, summoning her patience. Niccolo's words about being paid to be pleasant to the wealthy clients of the Clinico Silverio came to her mind, but she knew that this was not true of her relationship with Joanna. Kindness and patience were part of her stock-in-trade as a nurse and midwife, and had nothing to do with what she was paid. After all, Enrico had not paid her for her care of him this evening!

The plump maid put her head round the door. 'There is a gentleman to see you, *signorina*. Shall I ask him to come up to the apartment?'

'What? *No*!' she breathed, her heart giving a bound. Gentleman? Who could he possibly be except for Niccolo? 'I'll come down,' she told the girl, who nodded and disappeared.

The lift was engaged, so she skipped lightly down

the three flights of stairs to the bottom corridor, and breathlessly peeped over the stair-rail. Yes, there was no mistaking the tall figure standing beneath the shaded light. As soon as he saw her he came towards her in a swift movement, and caught hold of her hand.

'*Buona sera*, Pauline. My apologies for disturbing you. I told the maid not to wake you if you were asleep.' He glanced down at her dressing-gown and slippers. 'I felt that you would like to know about the two accident cases. . .'

'Oh, yes, of course I would!' She smiled, overjoyed to think that he had come to tell her. 'How is Mrs Partridge?'

'She has had a reduction of dislocated head of humerus, and has recovered from the anaesthetic. She's got an axillary pad in situ, and will have to wear a collar-and-cuff sling for a while.'

'And the concussion? Are there any effects?' asked Pauline anxiously.

'To judge by the furious arguments she has been having with Frank, I do not think there are any serious consequences from it.' His eyes twinkled.

'And—Enrico?'

'Ah, he is still in Theatre, for open reduction of fractured tib and fib and suturing of face.' He sighed. 'He will be a scarred but wiser young man in the future! He spoke of you when I saw him before he went into Theatre, and sends you his grateful thanks.'

'Did he? That was nice. Poor Enrico!'

'And I too have something to say to you—Paolina,' he went on, looking down at her, his eyes shadowed in the dim light. 'You were so good—such a calm, sensible nurse this evening, in a very difficult and

demanding situation—*magnifica*! I was glad that you
were with me. Thank you.'

'Any nurse worth the name would have done the
same,' she replied shyly, though his words were like
music in her ears. 'It's strange how we always rise to the
occasion in an emergency, isn't it? Let's say it was a good
thing that we were both on the spot when it happened!'

'Yes, you are right.'

His voice was low, and she thought how fascinating
the Florentine accent was—a soft and breathy dialect,
the language of Dante and generations of Tuscans who
had tilled the soil in this region and grown olives and
grapes for hundreds of years in the surrounding hills.

'I suppose I must now say goodnight and take my
leave of you, little Paolina,' he said, with a certain
reluctance that made her hold her breath. Careful, she
told herself.

'How long do you expect to stay in Florence,
Niccolo?'

Immediately the words were spoken, she regretted
them. She felt rather than saw his hesitation, and
almost a kind of defensiveness. Yet he was conven-
tionally polite in his reply.

'I hope not long. I expect to be occupied for a time
with sorting out a—a family matter.'

'I hope it works out well for you, Niccolo.' She
looked directly into his face, and he nodded briefly.

'Thank you. I hope so, too.'

'Goodnight, then.' She held out her hand before
turning to ascend the stairs. 'Thank you for coming
back to tell me about——'

'One moment, Paolina.'

There was an urgency in the way he spoke, the way
he seized her outstretched arm to detain her. Every

bone in her body seemed to melt under that darkly brooding gaze, that lofty nose that reminded her of the picture of Lorenzo il Magnifico, the great Medici ruler. Was she really standing here late at night in a Florentine *albergo* with this extraordinary doctor? Such things simply didn't happen in real life.

But this was not real life; this was Florence! She lowered her eyes, conscious of the dressing-gown and the thin cotton nightie beneath it. She stood with her shoulder against the wall, still and unresisting, while he slowly cupped a hand under her chin, tilting her face so that she had to look up at him. Then his face was nearer, so near that she involuntarily closed her eyes; she felt his lips brush her right cheek, and his breath was warm upon her skin. And then, in the Italian fashion, he kissed her left cheek.

She gave a sigh, and somehow her arms seemed to rise of their own volition to slide up around his neck. For a moment they held each other lightly and his mouth touched hers, sweetly, softly, as if not wanting to demand too much from the cool little English nurse who had made such an impression on him.

'*Buona notte*, little Paolina. Sleep well tonight, *cara mia*.'

And then he was gone, out into the street and to whatever duties demanded his time and attention. No arrangement had been made for them to meet again, but as she mounted the stairs on winged feet, her cheeks still glowing with the memory of his lips, the most extraordinary idea came into her mind.

She was face to face with her destiny. For her, Florence was not a foreign city, and she was no mere visitor to it. It was to become more important to her than anywhere else in the world.

CHAPTER FOUR

PAULINE fell at once into a deliciously deep sleep, though the night was broken as usual by Toni's feed in the small hours, when Joanna needed Pauline's presence and constant reassurance. Poor Stefano looked on anxiously, and quietly mentioned to Pauline that perhaps his wife should change to bottle-feeding, so that she could be relieved of the baby's constant demands on her.

'My mother or I myself could give the bottles, and I will hire a nursemaid to stay at Vernio,' he said, and much as Pauline was committed to promoting breast-feeding, she was beginning to think along the same lines.

Toni was over a month old, and thriving, while his mother was showing all the signs of clinical depression—tiredness, loss of appetite, insomnia, and a total lack of confidence in herself. Nevertheless Pauline knew of her determination to give her baby the ideal food, and felt that to change to formula milk would increase her sense of inadequacy as a mother.

When the night feed was finished, Pauline took Toni's cradle into her own room and they both settled to sleep soundly until brilliant sunshine poured in through the curtains; she had not closed the shutters against the light. She smiled and stretched luxuriously, revelling in the memory of Niccolo's late visit and the tender moment when he had kissed her. It filled her with soaring happiness and also a degree of apprehension. Had she read too much into his words and looks? Should she have responded in the way that she had?

I mustn't worry, she thought, remembering the way he had murmured her name, 'little Paolina'. He *must* want to see her again when his family commitments—whatever they were—had been dealt with, and no doubt all would be revealed and explained in due time. For the present she was content just to luxuriate in reliving that incredible kiss, and at the very thought of it she shivered with delight. . .

Toni's demands for his breakfast broke in on her daydreams, and she got out of bed to start the day's routine.

'Whatever shall I do without you, Pauline?' asked Joanna for the hundredth time, and once again Pauline tried to reassure her that she would be fine.

'Look, it's time you had some fresh air, Signora Sandrini! Let's take Toni out in his buggy on such a lovely day,' she suggested, and Stefano was all in favour. In fact, he suggested that the three of them took a packed lunch and had a picnic somewhere.

'What a good idea—don't you think so, Joanna?' smiled Pauline. 'I'll see the proprietress about the lunch, and maybe after we've had it you two could go off on your own for the afternoon and let me look after Toni. After all, we've only got tomorrow left, and——'

She checked herself on seeing Joanna's face fall, and her conscience nagged at her for not agreeing to go to Vernio with them. Even Niccolo had said that she should change her plans—but he was prejudiced against the Clinico Silverio.

If the truth were told, Pauline was longing to see Jenny again and get started on her new job. Although she was fond of Joanna, and adored Toni, she was finding the present situation very tiring. It was not that the work was hard—in fact, it was much easier than running a busy hospital ward or scrubbing up for an operation list—it was just that Joanna's dependence on her amounted to a round-the-clock responsibility, and she was seldom able to relax.

'I know, we'll go to the Boboli Gardens,' she said brightly. 'I've heard they're a picture in the spring.'

'Pauline is right,' said Stefano. 'We shall go by taxi to the Palazzo Pitti entrance, and spend an hour or two exploring the Giardini di Boboli. It will be a good place for a picnic, yes?'

A large basket of bread rolls, cheese, ham, tomatoes and peaches was brought to their room at eleven, and Pauline dressed Toni in a miniature suit for his airing.

Her spirits rose as the three of them entered the centuries-old pleasure park, with its shady arbours and twisty paths that emerged from a maze of formal clipped hedges to give panoramic views of the city from rising ground. Stefano and Joanna walked arm-in-arm while Pauline pushed the buggy.

'Oh, just look at that hideous marble dwarf riding a turtle!' shuddered Joanna, with a grimace at the fat, naked statue grinning at the passers-by from his niche. Stefano laughed and defended him.

'That fine fellow was the court jester of Cosimo Medici, who designed these gardens for his Spanish wife—perhaps to make her feel happy, eh, my Giovanna?' he teased, giving his wife's arm an affectionate squeeze.

Pauline thought what a nice man he was, and she longed for Joanna to be more responsive and cheerful. She tried to interest her in the grottoes, and the lake with its fountains and swans. Did poor Stefano realise what difficulties lay ahead? she wondered uneasily.

When they had decided on a sunny spot for their picnic, looking down on an avenue of cypresses and Roman statuary, Pauline made the couple sit down while she took charge of the food basket. She was about to start unpacking it when a man and woman walking up the avenue towards them caught her eye.

She stopped what she was doing, her hand gripping the curved handle of the basket in sudden tension.

No, it couldn't be. But, yes, there he was.

'Is something the matter, Signorina Pauline?' asked Stefano, and at the same time Joanna also saw the couple.

'Look over there, Pauline, isn't that our doctor again? Do you see?'

Pauline certainly did see, and her heart had given the usual wild leap. It was as if she was destined to run into Niccolo everywhere she went in this city of magic. She sat riveted to the spot while he came nearer, as if summoned by her wish. They were almost face to face. . .

Only this time he had a young woman on his arm, a dark-eyed, pale-skinned, very slim girl, who was talking rapidly and forcefully to him as he inclined his dark head towards her.

When he saw Pauline and the Sandrinis he stopped dead in his tracks, staring at them and at Toni's buggy, equally taken by surprise. Pauline was aware of several different impressions at once, and saw that he was not pleased this time, for he did not smile at her but glanced quickly at the girl by his side, who gave Pauline a frankly hostile look. He opened his mouth as if to speak, and then closed it again.

Pauline was never more thankful for the discipline instilled by her nursing training; it stood her in good stead at this extremely awkward moment. The girl with Niccolo, whoever she was, clearly had a relationship with him that went back a good deal further than her own brief acquaintance.

Was she a girlfriend who had no intention of giving him up? Could she be the reason for his hasty return to Florence? If so, it must be a very pressing matter, to cause him to break his year's contract to serve on Mr Mason's surgical team at Beltonshaw, even if only temporarily. All sorts of possibilities whirled into Pauline's head during that fraught moment in the Boboli Gardens.

Mastering her emotions and summoning up her cool common sense, Pauline felt that her chief priority right now was to avoid embarrassing this man any further. She would have to be calmly, casually friendly, so as not to give the girl any grounds for suspicion. So she moistened her dry lips and smiled pleasantly.

'Why, Dr Ghiberti, *buongiorno*.'

But she had reckoned without Joanna.

'Oh, Dr Ghiberti, what a nice surprise! How are you? This is my husband, Stefano, and of course you know my wonderful friend Pauline. I have told Stefano how you saved my life in hospital, and came to my rescue on the plane. Won't you introduce us to your charming friend?'

Somehow or other Pauline kept her expression neutral while she observed Niccolo's reaction to this greeting, unusually animated for Joanna. He threw her a brief, apologetic glance as he replied politely, addressing Joanna as *signora* and nodding to Stefano.

He avoided introducing the girl, and enquired about Toni's progress.

Before Joanna could reply, the girl cut in sharply, speaking in rapid Italian. 'Don't introduce *me* to your fine English friends, Niccolo!' she sneered. 'Think how humiliating it would be! But remember that it was not *I* who asked you to come rushing home!'

Her angry words were uttered with such vehemence that the Sandrinis were as much taken aback as Pauline, who saw Niccolo stiffen and roll his eyes heavenwards, as if in barely controlled exasperation.

'Annalisa, *please*!' he muttered under his breath.

The girl turned her unsmiling face on the three of them, and flashed Pauline a particularly suspicious look.

Pauline stared coolly back at her, as she might have done to a defiant student midwife on duty. They had done nothing to warrant such an outburst from a complete stranger. Yet her professional observation of this girl noted that there were dark smudges beneath the baleful dark eyes, making them look enormous in the thin face framed by fluffy dark brown hair, and the thinly compressed mouth had a pinched look.

There was trouble here, that much was clear, and Niccolo put a restraining arm around Annalisa's rigid shoulders, showing quite astonishing forbearance towards her unsociable behaviour.

It's nothing to do with me, thought Pauline, and decided that her best course of action would be to allow him to make a speedy escape. She forced a polite smile.

'We had better not detain you, Dr Ghiberti. As you can see, we are about to have a picnic lunch. Nice to have seen you again—*buongiorno*!'

She turned away and applied her attention to unpacking the basket, not wanting him to suspect the turmoil in her heart and trembling limbs.

The girl clung to Niccolo in a way that would have seemed very childish if Pauline had not sensed a pathetic defensiveness about her. Poor Annalisa—she must be desperately unsure of herself, she thought detachedly.

The Sandrinis were bewildered, but Stefano quickly took his cue from Pauline, and gave a politely dismissive nod to the couple.

'*Buongiorno, Dottore e signorina.*'

But Niccolo did not immediately walk on. He apparently debated within himself for a moment, and then abruptly stepped forward to say a few words to Pauline in a low tone. Annalisa still hung on to his arm, but he faced Pauline squarely, and she could not look away from the troubled eyes that held her as he spoke in English.

'I am so sorry, Sister Pauline. This is not as I intended, you understand.'

She heard herself whisper, 'I understand.' Even though she didn't.

His brief, grateful smile touched her heart.

'Enjoy the rest of your stay in Florence. And. . .' He hesitated just for a moment as Annalisa waited impatiently. 'And thank you.'

It was an unmistakable farewell. Taking Annalisa's arm firmly in his, he continued along the cypress avenue without a backward glance. Pauline willed herself to remain outwardly calm as she proceeded to attend to the lunch, but it cost her an effort that was not lost on her friends.

'My God! I don't think much of Dr Ghiberti's choice,

do you?' asked Joanna. 'What manners! What on earth can he see in her?'

Pauline shrugged, hoping that the Sandrinis would not notice that she was blinking back tears as she handed out plates and linen napkins.

'I do not know, *cara mia*. Your doctor seems to be caught in a trap,' replied Stefano thoughtfully.

'But that's terrible! Oh, Pauline, do you think she's the reason he's come back to Florence?' asked Joanna.

Pauline could not trust herself to speak, but Stefano replied with a wry smile, 'More likely the reason that he fled to England!'

'And now she's brought him back,' conjectured Joanna. 'Poor Niccolo—I'd have thought he'd have more sense.'

Pauline remembered Annalisa's insistence that she had not asked Niccolo to come back. Yet she could have appealed to his conscience and forced him to make his own decision to return. . .

Joanna's thoughts were following the same track, because her next words voiced Pauline's own reaction.

'Heavens, Pauline, you don't think she's—she couldn't be *pregnant*?'

Again Stefano answered, having noted Pauline's shock and dismay; he guessed something of what she was feeling.

'No, she is much too thin. And it is not our affair. Ah, Pauline, this crusty bread is good, and we have peaches for dessert—*delizioso*!'

'Eat up, Joanna. It's important that you do,' urged Pauline, grateful for the change of subject. What a dear Stefano was, she thought.

As he tucked his napkin under his plump chin, he leaned towards Pauline and made a quiet observation.

'I saw the look the doctor gave you, Pauline, and I know which girl he would prefer if he had a choice—and it is not the thin one, no?'

She could have kissed him, and hoped with all her heart that Joanna's depression would lift and allow them both to share the mutual happiness of parenthood after such an unfortunate start.

As they were finishing the picnic Toni woke up and announced in his usual way that it was his turn. Pauline tried to persuade Joanna to give him the breast there in the gardens, facing away from the avenue and shielded by Stefano's broad back.

'Italian mothers haven't got this silly attitude towards something so natural,' she said. 'I saw a mother feeding her baby in the *piazza* on Wednesday evening, and nobody took any notice at all.'

But Joanna had been thoroughly put off by the disapproving air passengers, and insisted that they return to the Pitti Palace, where she could feed Toni in the ladies' room there. Afterwards Stefano readily accepted Pauline's offer to take charge of Toni while he and Joanna spent the afternoon together.

'We go for a romantic interlude, yes?' He smiled happily.

Pauline gave him a saucy wink, and promised not to turn up at the apartment for at least two hours.

She pushed the buggy through the streets and squares of Florence, glad of the privacy which allowed her to rearrange her thoughts about Niccolo in the light of this latest encounter. When she found herself in the Piazza del Duomo, the great cathedral square, with its Baptistery of St John and the gracious four-teenth-century palaces, she saw the olive-green vans outside one of the entrances. Of course! This must be the headquarters of the amazing Brotherhood that not only manned the ambulances but took consolation and tender care to those troubled in body and mind.

On an impulse she took the buggy into the cool dimness of the cathedral and knelt down briefly to ask for guidance and good sense—not only for herself but for Niccolo Ghiberti, and the parents of the little baby boy sleeping beside her as she prayed.

And for the unhappy Annalisa. . .

On Saturday morning they all got up early, and Pauline helped Joanna to sort out her belongings and Toni's before she hastily finished packing her own clothes.

Two taxis had been ordered, and the Bandrinis' arrived first. While Stefano and the driver pushed their luggage into every available space Pauline took an emotional farewell of Joanna, who confessed that she was dreading being marooned with old Signora Sandrini at Vernio. She begged Pauline to change her mind at this eleventh hour, and come with them.

Pauline shook her head firmly, and made a last effort to bolster up Joanna's wilting self-confidence.

'If you had me with you all the time you'd never learn to stand on your own feet, love. *Do* try to enjoy your lovely baby—and don't spoil your happiness by worrying so much. Stefano worships you—you're so lucky!'

She kissed the tearstained face of the patient who had become a friend.

'We'll keep in touch, and you must let me know how you go on. Here's the telephone number of the Clinico Silverio, so give me a ring and tell me how well you're coping, all right?'

She waved after the departing taxi and wished that

she felt as optimistic as she'd sounded. Joanna should be so happy, with a beautiful baby, a devoted husband and no financial worries—thanks to Stefano's efforts at the time of Toni's birth to put his business on a sound footing. Pauline wondered how much of her friend's anxiety was aggravated by the prospect of living permanently abroad, away from her own family and friends in England. Marriage to a foreign national was a big step to take. . .

And one which she, Pauline, was never likely to be faced with, she told herself as she got into her taxi and set off on the road to Fiesole and the Clinico Silverio.

CHAPTER FIVE

PAULINE sat back in the taxi, determined to enjoy the drive, which was certainly impressive. Once out of the city the road climbed in a zig-zag course upwards through steep terrain dotted here and there with elegant villas. At intervals there would be a gap in the hills and she would get an unexpected view of Florence and the Arno valley. It was a superb prospect, but not sufficiently absorbing to keep her thoughts away from either the Sandrinis or Niccolo and the dreadful Annalisa.

What *was* his commitment to the girl that made him tolerate such awful behaviour? Were they engaged? Living together? Could Stefano have been right when he'd hinted that Niccolo's decision to spend a year in England might have been a bid for freedom—an attempt to escape from a relationship that had become burdensome? If so, how had Annalisa persuaded him to break his contract and return to her ill-tempered domination?

All these thoughts churned around in Pauline's head without coming to any satisfactory conclusion. That Niccolo was a kind and capable doctor there was no doubt, and it was *she*, Pauline, whom he had sought out in Florence. Why else should he have returned to the *albergo* on Wednesday evening after their involvement with the Partridges and Enrico? And the kiss that had sent her heart soaring as never before—surely that had been no casual impulse? She realised that her

memories of Giorgio had been finally eclipsed in that
moment. . . .

In spite of such a short acquaintance, Pauline felt
that she knew something of Niccolo's character, and
on one point she was quite certain: if he had a moral
obligation of any kind that went against his own wishes,
even against his happiness, he would never try to forget
it or set it aside. He would stand by his commitment
and not look for a way of escape. And Annalisa was
obviously just such an obligation.

So she might as well stop daydreaming and go for
this change of scenery and company that the Clinico
Silverio offered, away from the city that had cast such
a spell over her. There was nothing she could do about
Niccolo's problem, however much she might wish to
help him.

Her thoughts were jerked back to the present when
the taxi veered off along a stony track and descended
a little way before turning a sharp bend. Pauline's eyes
widened at the sight of a large, attractive two-storey
building in the honey-coloured stone typical of this
district.

Shaped like an 'E' without the middle bar, it
enclosed a central paved courtyard with a fountain and
the goddess Diana in stone. It did not look in the least
like a hospital, and stood in its own walled grounds
with shrubs and flowering gorse against dark trees in
the middle distance. Although the sun was hot, the
altitude ensured a cool breeze, and Pauline glimpsed
the blue-green sparkle of a swimming-pool edged with
a marble terrace on which half a dozen figures lounged
in reclining chairs.

The taxi passed under a rounded archway and pulled
up before a porticoed entrance. A young woman

appeared, her body rounded in mid-pregnancy, and hurried joyfully down a few steps to the taxi as Pauline emerged from it.

'Pauline!'

'Jenny! Oh, it's good to see you at last—and don't you look marvellous! Maternity suits you!'

They kissed and embraced closely. 'Welcome to the Clinico Silverio, Pauline. I've been counting the days!'

Pauline's spirits rose as she hugged her friend. 'No, don't you *dare* touch the luggage, Jenny,' she warned, and, picking up her one large suitcase, she followed Jenny into a cool reception hall, where there was a desk and a life-size replica of the Medici Venus in the Uffizi Gallery.

'This looks super, just like a four-star hotel!' she enthused, looking around her. 'Or perhaps a convent, with those arched cloisters running round the court-yard! I can't wait to see everything.'

'It's a real hotch-potch of a hospital, with all kinds of different treatments for different patients,' Jenny told her. 'We follow the holistic approach here, and try to treat the whole person, not just their symptoms.'

'What sort of patients do you take?' asked Pauline, remembering Niccolo's dismissive comments.

'Selected ones, mostly—those we really think we can help. Quite a few psychiatric and psychosomatic problems for Dr Luongo to deal with—including detoxifications, who have to be hand-held through the hell of withdrawal. Diet plays a big part here, and we place a lot of importance on it. Riccardo insists that we are what we eat! So the accent's on freshness, high fibre, low sugar and cholesterol—all those things. I'll take you to your room first of all, Pauline, so leave your case here for the time being, and come this way.'

'And the treatments?' asked Pauline curiously as Jenny led her down a long corridor and up a circular staircase to the upper floor.

'All kinds. Acupuncture, homeopathy, osteopathy, aromatherapy——'

'Steady on, Jenny, this is a foreign language to me, remember,' Pauline cut in. 'All these alternative remedies and diets and what-have-you, we wouldn't even have considered them at Beltonshaw, would we?'

She felt a little awkward at expressing her scepticism to her friend, but Jenny laughed good-humouredly.

'Ah, I see we'll have to convert you! We *do* have conventional surgery and medicine, of course, and we sometimes switch treatments if they don't appear to be working. We get quite a few patients sent to us by orthodox practitioners, to see if we can do anything when all else has failed—as a last resort, you could say! And *all* treatments are combined with counselling; that never stops.

'Violetta—that's Dr Luongo, our resident psychiatrist—leads a team which includes a priest and a nice little unshockable nun, Sister Agnello. But we *all* make a point of listening to patients, letting them talk through their problems and pointing them in the right direction. We try to avoid giving direct advice, as they usually need to work out the answers for themselves. Put it this way, Pauline—it's no good operating on a peptic ulcer if the patient then goes back to the stressful situation that caused the ulcer in the first place, don't you agree?'

'Mmm, yes, I used to feel like that at Beltonshaw General sometimes,' admitted Pauline, remembering her days on Female Surgical. 'But you can't change people's circumstances, can you?'

'No, but you can sometimes change their mental attitude—the way they react to those circumstances,' answered Jenny seriously. 'You'd be surprised at the damage done by resentment, bitterness, old grudges and jealousies from way back that need facing up to and healing. We can help a lot with that. Not in every case, of course, but our success rate is quite high, to judge by the number who come back to tell us! For instance, we've had some good results with anorexics, and desperate parents have brought girls here who haven't responded to conventional hospital treatment.'

She stopped outside a door which she opened and waved Pauline inside.

'This is your room. I expect you'll want to freshen up a bit now, and then we'll have coffee and talk some more. Lunch is at twelve-thirty, first sitting, and I'm warning you—it's communal living here. That means we all share the same dining-room—staff and ambulant patients together, family-style! Coffee in about twenty minutes, all right?'

Pauline sat down on the side of the single divan bed with its flower-patterned duvet, and looked round at the pale cream walls and polished wood floor with a sand-coloured rug. There was a small wardrobe and dressing-table, and a low bench seat ran along one wall beneath the window. It was a clean, uncluttered room where she would have space and privacy; after the week at the *albergo* with Joanna and Toni it was very welcome, and yet there was still a nagging doubt at the back of her mind as to whether she should have gone to Vernio with them.

She confided these thoughts to Jenny when they took coffee in a sunny corner or the courtyard.

'Oh, Pauline, I'm glad you *didn't*. We need you

here!' emphasised her friend. 'I'm too far on now to stand around in Theatre for three hours on op days, and Riccardo was getting really worried. We have a good theatre staff nurse, Kitty O'Hare, but she's Irish-American and has to go back to the States at the end of May. There just aren't that many good, all-round theatre sisters who are willing to live in and take over the nursing of post-op patients as required. We just went wild when we got your phone call, I can tell you!'

As they chatted they were joined by a sad-faced girl of about eighteen whose emaciated appearance frankly shocked Pauline. Her limbs were like sticks and her hollow eyes stared dully out of a face so thin that the skull bones could be seen below the pale parchment skin. Her long, light brown hair hung down lifelessly over bony shoulders.

'Hi, Nina! Draw up a seat and meet our new member of staff,' said Jenny easily. 'Hang on, I'll just pop in and get a cushion.'

She went indoors, and Nina stared suspiciously at Pauline, who forced a smile and introduced herself in Italian.

'I'm Pauline, and pleased to meet you—er, Nina.'

'I doubt it,' replied the girl in English, not returning the smile.

'Pardon? What do you doubt, Nina?' asked Pauline, still trying to adjust to such a pathetic sight as the girl presented.

'That you're pleased to meet me. Nobody else is. Who wants to meet a nutcase? I'm just taking up a place here that could be used for somebody more deserving,' said Nina, pressing her thin lips together as she lowered her angular bottom on to the seat where Jenny had just placed a couple of soft cushions.

'Now, Nina, you know that's nonsense,' said Jenny, with a glance at Pauline.

'Don't think that you have to talk to me. I don't respond to reason or common sense,' Nina warned Pauline with unnerving directness, and Pauline was at a loss as to how to respond to a person whose self-esteem was so low as to be non-existent.

'It's Sister Agnello's literature lesson this afternoon, isn't it?' said Jenny, pouring out a third cup of coffee and producing a chocolate biscuit bar which she put beside Nina's cup. The girl's flat eyes brightened a little.

'Yes, back to good old Dante and his *Inferno*—and the damned spirits in hell,' she replied with gloomy relish. '*There's* a man who understood—somebody I can relate to.'

This girl is on the defensive, thought Pauline. She's trying to warn me off. Without stopping to think, she answered gently, 'I was always taught that hell is a state of mind and that nobody has to go there unless they choose it. If we choose hell instead of happiness that's up to us, but we don't have to.'

A flicker of interest showed on Nina's gaunt face.

'Are you a shrink?' she asked bluntly. 'Or a nun in disguise?'

'Neither. I'm the new theatre sister, actually,' smiled Pauline over the top of her cup.

'Oho! You'll be bringing in the money to run the place, then,' observed Nina cynically.

Pauline was baffled, and Jenny attempted to explain.

'Nina doesn't mince her words, Pauline, as you'll have gathered. What she means is that our surgical cases provide the main source of income for the clinic. On the whole it's pretty straightforward surgery—a few gastrectomies and cholecystectomies, plus gynae and the usual minor excisions and repairs—hernias, varicose veins and so on.'

'For which they pay an arm and a leg,' added Nina.

'We have to charge, of course—can't run a place like this on fresh air,' agreed Jenny with cheerful frankness. 'You could say we follow Robin Hood, and use the rich to subsidise the less well-off. Quite a number are treated on a pay-what-you-can basis, and in fact we live on a knife-edge—but we love it, and we're beginning to build up a reputation. Come on, I'll show you round before lunch. Excuse us, Nina, dear, won't you?'

When the girl was out of earshot, Jenny told Pauline something of her history.

'Anorexia nervosa is a form of depression that affects young women, mainly, and it's usually a family situation that starts it off. Nina's a particularly sad case because she's highly intelligent and should be having a great time at university now, not stuck here. Somehow her parents have made her feel inadequate, and she's reacted by starving herself to punish both herself and them. And she's certainly succeeded in driving them frantic, poor things!

'We try to avoid gastric tube-feeding if we possibly can, and we do our best to get the girls to communicate with us by one means or another—talking, writing, drawing and painting, pottery, music—anything that interests them. We forget about diets, and let them have what they'll eat—chocolate, syrupy milkshakes, biscuits, anything edible!'

'And is Nina making any progress?' asked Pauline, aghast at this waste of youth and talent.

'On and off. Sister Agnello's very good with her, and gets her to write down her thoughts as poetry, which they then discuss. But Nina knows that if she doesn't gain weight over the weekend she'll have to be put to bed and tube-fed, which we consider failure on our part. Still, if it saves her life. . .' She sighed and shrugged.

Even on her first day Pauline became intrigued by the holistic approach to health, and the emphasis placed on positive thinking. She discovered a serene and friendly atmosphere about the place; nobody was too busy to sit down and listen to problems, great or small. The food was simple but delicious, with lots of fresh vegetables and fruit, thick home-made minestrone soups, beans, plump sun-ripened tomatoes, cheese and olive oil. Dark, coarse-textured Tuscan bread was served at all meals, which were taken in an airy dining-room with circular tables of different sizes.

When Pauline next saw Nina, she asked if she could arrange the girl's long hair in a braid, starting at the crown of her head. The result was quite striking, and even Nina had to admit that it looked nice.

'Beauty therapy is *so* important for women,' commented Jenny later. 'I give sessions on skin- and hair-care, using basic cleansing creams and moisturisers—and my best beauty tip is a real bargain. Drink a litre of plain water every day!'

It was Riccardo who introduced Pauline to the surgical suite, which consisted of six adjacent single rooms on a ground floor corridor, with an operating theatre at one end and a sister's office at the other.

'Normally there are two operating lists each week,' he told her. 'Surgeons come from other hospitals to operate on their own patients, and I do a fair bit of straightforward surgery myself—and also act as anaes-

thetist for visiting surgeons. You will be both theatre
sister and sister-in-charge of the surgical suite.'

'Wonderful! I'll really enjoy following the patients
through after surgery,' said Pauline with enthusiasm.
'The best of both worlds! What other staff are there?'

'Nurse O'Hare is very capable, and we have an excel-
lent night staff,' he told her. 'Jenny has been doing a
lot of the theatre work, but it's too much for her now.
There are a couple of good auxiliaries, and a wizard
male theatre orderly, who can turn his hand to anything
mechanical and knows the likes and dislikes of every
visiting surgeon.'

Pauline nodded, impressed by the gleaming cleanli-
ness of the small but well-designed theatre and the tidy
office with its computer and neatly printed files on
each patient.

'We have our own small laboratory, and a refriger-
ator next to the theatre for the storage of blood,' went
on Riccardo. 'All our operations are booked cases. We
don't do emergencies here, so our patients are X-rayed
and cross-matched before admission—usually at Santa
Maria Nuova, or the nearest large hospital to where
they live.'

He then introduced her to the four patients currently
in the suite. Only one, a store manageress who
had had a mastectomy two days previously, needed
skilled nursing care. Three men awaited surgery on
Monday—one of them a popular footballer, who was
in for a meniscectomy following a knee injury. An
embarrassed garage owner with haemorrhoids was in
the room next to him, and the third was a retired
businessman for trans-urethral prostatectomy.

At her earliest opportunity Pauline made a point of
sitting down and chatting with each of the four in turn,

introducing herself to them and their relatives, and answering any queries they wanted to make.

Already she was convinced that this had been a good career move, and threw herself whole-heartedly into her new life. Beltonshaw seemed as far away as the moon, and if thoughts of Niccolo occasionally intruded, she dealt with them ruthlessly. A man with a moral obligation to another woman was a no-go area.

The three operations were performed on Monday morning, starting with the footballer's knee. Jenny scrubbed up as theatre sister for this while Pauline looked on. Kitty O'Hare scrubbed for the prostatectomy, and Pauline made her début as theatre sister for the excision of piles. All three cases were straightforward, and the list was finished well before midday.

Pauline felt that she had acquitted herself well, and would be able to undertake the next full list, which meant that there would be no further need for Jenny to go into the theatre—much to Riccardo's relief. Kitty remained on duty that afternoon while Pauline took a few hours off, returning for the evening shift at five.

It was at dinner that evening that Pauline met Maria, a rather intense girl, who was introduced by Jenny as an ex-patient who now worked two or three evenings as a voluntary helper.

'You'd never believe that Maria was totally hooked on tranquillisers last year, would you?' whispered Jenny. 'We had a simply awful time with her! Now she works as a secretary in Florence, and shares a super apartment with two other girls. She's become a friend of Nina's, and puts up with a fair amount of flak from her—but Maria seems to be unsnubbable!'

Pauline found it hard to believe that the pretty,

chatty Maria could ever have been a depressed drug addict, and asked her about her present life and work.

'I just had to get away from my parents, even though they love me and want the best for me,' Maria told her. 'When they began to have problems with their marriage, I thought it was because they had such a stupid daughter—they're very clever, you see—and I blamed myself for letting them down. Dr Luongo and Dr Alberi did wonders for me, and now I live my own life and everything's fine.'

Pauline was intrigued. 'And why do you come back here to visit patients like Nina?'

'I want to help others in return for all the help I was given,' replied Maria earnestly. 'After being in such a muddle myself, I know what hell it can be! Actually, one of the girls I live with is giving me a lot of anxiety at present. I'm *sure* she has the same problem as Nina, but she won't admit that she's ill and needs help.' She shrugged helplessly. 'But there you are, she's a Ghiberti, and they're all so proud!'

Pauline was immediately alerted by the mention of that name.

'This girl you mention, Maria—does she have any relatives?' she asked.

'Only a brother now, and he's a doctor—but even *he* can't reason with her,' answered Maria with a shake of her head.

Pauline's interest was now definitely aroused. 'And does this doctor—her brother—does he work in Florence?' she asked, trying to keep her voice casual.

'Yes, apart from when his work takes him away. At present he's working as a locum in Pronto Soccorso at Santa Maria Nuova.'

At this point Riccardo, who was sitting with Jenny

at the same table, came in on the conversation.

'It's a tragic story, Pauline. Both their parents were killed outright in the most horrendous car crash on the *autostrada*. They were on their way to meet their son at the airport. He'd only just got his medical degree, the same year as myself, so it must be four years ago.'

'Yes, Annalisa was in her first year at University,' added Maria.

'*Annalisa*!' cried Pauline, and her fork clattered down on to the floor. Jenny and Maria stared at her.

'Are you all right, Pauline?' asked Jenny. 'Do you know the Ghibertis?'

'Er—yes, I think I do, in a way,' stammered Pauline. 'Is his name—er—Niccolo?'

'Yes! However do you know *him*?' Jenny was both surprised and intrigued, especially as Pauline's astonishment was giving way to unmistakable joy.

'I met him when he came over to work at Beltonshaw General earlier this year,' she explained, her blue-grey eyes alight with the thrill of this discovery.

'Good heavens! Did he go *there*?' exclaimed Riccardo.

'Yes, he came back only last week,' said Maria.

'*Why* exactly did he come back?' Pauline asked eagerly. 'He was supposed to be on a year's exchange scheme, doing a surgical registrarship.'

There was a pause, and Maria looked down at her plate.

'For heaven's sake, *tell* me, Maria!' begged Pauline, throwing all reticence to the winds, so desperately did she need to know the reason behind the mystery of Niccolo's movements and behaviour. And if Annalisa was his *sister*. . .

'All right, I will tell you, if you really want to know,'

said Maria reluctantly, glancing round the table. 'And if you promise never to tell Annalisa. . .' She paused while the three of them listened, and took a deep breath.

'I wrote to him,' she confessed. 'Elena—that's the other girl in the apartment—she and I agreed that he ought to be told that we were very worried about her health. She was losing weight and not eating enough to keep a sparrow alive. To do him credit, he took notice of me and came back straight away. The trouble is that Annalisa refuses to see a psychiatrist, and spends all her time at the apartment since she lost her job. And she is getting worse. It is a great worry for him, and Elena and I have to keep out of the way when he comes to see her. They argue and shout—it is terrible!'

'What a tragedy,' remarked Riccardo seriously. 'I do not think that Annalisa has ever got over the shock of their parents' death. First she dropped out of university, and then there was a mad, passionate affair with some guy who threw her over—probably because she is so neurotic.'

'Wasn't there some talk of her attempting suicide at one time?' asked Jenny.

'Gossip, Jenny!' he warned. 'I do not think that Annalisa would ever throw herself off the Ponte Vecchio. She just plays on Niccolo's fears and manipulates him for all she's worth, I am afraid.'

'What she needs is to come here for some no-nonsense counselling,' said Jenny. 'Violetta Luongo could work out a programme for her.'

'Oh, yes, that would be ideal!' agreed Pauline, her eyes sparkling. She could hardly take in this revelation. His *sister*! The knowledge put everything in a new and exciting light.

'No chance,' said Riccardo, shaking his head. 'Niccolo would never agree to it. He's highly suspicious of private clinics like ours.'

Pauline remembered Niccolo's words about pandering to wealthy hypochondriacs, and kept a discreet silence, though inwardly she rejoiced at what she now saw as an explanation of his attitude regarding Annalisa. Of course he would feel a tremendous sense of obligation towards his younger sister when they had both been so disastrously orphaned by such a fearful stroke of fate!

And there was no reason now why she should not look for a chance to help them both. No amount of unsocial behaviour on Annalisa's part would offend her, because she now looked upon the girl as a patient in need of her understanding as a nurse. And as Niccolo's sister!

She became aware that Jenny was observing her closely, and she smiled back, unaware of how openly she revealed her new-found happiness. Jenny pursed her lips doubtfully, and after the meal she beckoned Pauline out into the courtyard where they coould talk without being overheard.

'Pauline, dear, you're showing the stars in your eyes,' she said affectionately. 'Now, you won't go and fall in love with Niccolo Ghiberti, will you? I've never met him personally, but according to Riccardo he's so tied up with that sister of his that it makes him bad news for nice girls like you. Honestly, love, she manipulates him and plays on his sense of family pride. The Ghibertis are fearfully arrogant, like so many of these old Florentine families, and would never admit to any kind of mental unbalance in their noble blood!'

Pauline gave her a radiant smile. 'Thanks, Jenny. I

know you mean well, but I'm afraid you're already too late,' she confessed, thinking that she might as well own up. 'As soon as I first met Niccolo at Beltonshaw, there was this special, indescribable something between us that I haven't felt since Giorgio——'

'Yes, and look what happened with *him*,' Jenny pointed out.

'Oh, Niccolo's so different—I know he is,' Pauline insisted, and went on to describe the scene on the plane and then the evening in Florence and the way he had reacted to the street accident.

'I feel sure that he was looking out for me that evening, Jenny, even if against his better judgement,' she confided. 'Although he was secretive about the reason he'd returned to Florence, he came back to the *albergo* late that night, and——'

'Threw himself at your feet and swore undying devotion?' prompted Jenny with a grin.

'Call me an idiot if you like, but he showed that he felt the—the attraction too,' muttered Pauline, not willing to tell even her best friend about the sweetness of that goodnight kiss. 'I was so happy, Jenny—but then when I next met him in the Boboli Gardens, with this unfriendly girl who was so rude to me and the Sandrinis, I thought she must be a girlfriend or somebody he was committed to in some way. You can imagine how awful I felt—I had no idea that she was his *sister*! Oh, Jenny, you don't know how happy that makes me! Thank you! *Thank you*!'

And she threw her arms around her friend and hugged her then and there.

'Steady on, love, you'll frighten the baby! I can see that I'm wasting my breath on you,' said Jenny when Pauline released her. 'But don't you see, love, it's *because* she's his sister that she'll always be around, spoiling things for him and fighting off all rivals for his attention. She can't be sent packing, not like a tiresome girlfriend. Family ties are terribly strong among these Florentines—oh, Pauline, stay away from a disaster area!'

For answer Pauline just smiled, and said she had a proposition to put to Jenny and Riccardo.

'If Annalisa is as ill as Maria says—and she looked shockingly thin and miserable when I saw her last week—wouldn't it be best for her to come here for a while and get properly sorted out?'

'Yes, of course it would, Pauline. I said so at the table just now, but we can't go out and kidnap patients! Nobody can be forced to accept treatment, and if that haughty Ghiberti girl refuses to see a specialist recommended by her brother, you can bet your sweet life she won't be prepared to come *here* on a voluntary basis—admitting that she needs help.'

'But if Niccolo were to persuade her. . .' went on Pauline in a rush of eagerness.

'Mmm, I can't see him doing that if he disapproves of hospitals like ours. He'd look on it as an admission of failure. Hey, what kind of plan are you hatching, Pauline?' Jenny asked curiously.

'Just answer this question, Jenny. If I was able to persuade Niccolo to convince his sister that the Clinico Silverio would be her best bet, and to get her to agree to a trial period of, say, three weeks, would you and Riccardo be prepared to take her on?'

Jenny looked sceptical. 'I don't know, Pauline. Three weeks isn't long. It can take three months to get results with some of these stubborn anorexics. We've had Nina for over a month, and she's only just beginning to respond—you can see that she has a very long way to go. In any case, how on earth do you think you can influence Dr Ghiberti, if you don't mind my asking?'

'I don't know yet, Jenny, but I certainly intend to try,' vowed Pauline. 'I can be stubborn, too, and when I really make up my mind I'll do anything—and I mean *anything*—to achieve my goal! So if I can get Annalisa here, by fair means or foul, would you be prepared to take her on?'

Jenny shook her head in disbelief of her friend's powers of persuasion, but agreed that if Annalisa would come to the Clinico Silverio, she and Riccardo would rise to the challenge.

'But honestly, Pauline, love, I'd keep out of their way if I were you. You're heading for trouble, in my opinion.'

'Thanks, Jenny, you're a pal,' replied Pauline, and returned to her duties in the surgical suite, where the three post-op patients needed her attention.

That first week at the clinic passed quickly, and Pauline loved the varied nature of her work. She spent much of her off-duty time with Nina, and was fascinated by Sister Agnello's literature lessons, which were really counselling sessions in disguise.

The little nun discussed language and poetry covering a whole range of human experience and emotion while studiously avoiding the subject of food and eating, though fruit drinks and ice-creams would mysteriously appear on the table where they sat, along with the chocolate bars and sweet biscuits to which Sister Agnello was partial.

It was an education to watch the casual way in which

Nina was beguiled into taking a bite or a lick or a sip while concentrating her mind on the finer points of rhyme and metre. Pauline asked Nina if she might read some of her verses, and found them highly imaginative though heartrendingly sad, giving an insight into the girl's feelings of inadequacy while revealing her longing to be normal.

Making friends with Maria was Pauline's next step, and through her to gain admittance to the apartment which she shared with Annalisa and Elena. After considering whether to take Maria into her confidence, she decided against it.

The girl had already proved herself to be somewhat interfering by writing to Niccolo, even though her intentions had been good.

Pauline hit on the idea of asking Maria to help her choose a birthday present for Jenny, and arranged to meet her in the Piazza del Duomo on Saturday, her day off at the end of her first week at the clinic. It should not be difficult to find an excuse to visit the apartment, she thought, where hopefully she might meet Annalisa, and by tact and diplomacy begin to build up some sort of a relationship with Niccolo's difficult sister.

It was a precarious plan, which could easily misfire, but Pauline was determined not to be discouraged. And if she missed Annalisa on this occasion she would at least know where to find the apartment another time. She had no intention of giving up. The certainty she had felt that night on the balcony of the Albergo Roccia Bianca had never really left her; she believed that her destiny lay here, and was inextricably linked with Niccolo Ghiberti.

*   *   *

When Saturday came, Pauline chose her clothes carefully, aiming at a casually neat appearance—a nurse off duty. She rejected a lacy blouse in favour of a plain white short-sleeved cotton shirt, and decided on the denim skirt again, now held at the waist by a plaited leather belt. Her legs were bare, and she wore white sandals with low heels for easy walking. A pretty necklace of blue china beads with matching ear-studs completed the outfit.

A supplies van from Fiesole called each morning at the clinic, and Pauline travelled back on it to the town, where she boarded a bus going down into Florence. She settled herself to look out of the window at the burgeoning Tuscan countryside shimmering beneath a cloudless blue sky—a unique landscape of lush cultivation dotted with straight, tall cypresses and ilex, a fruitful, fertile soil little changed by the centuries.

As the bus descended the zig-zag winding road she felt the heat increasing. How wonderful to spend the summer months in the cooler hilly region, with Florence only a bus-ride away!

When Maria appeared in the *piazza*, Pauline suggested that they went for coffee in one of the flowery *trattorie* with pavement tables that bordered the square, to discuss where they should go shopping. She also ordered ice-creams for them both.

'The Mercato Nuovo has got some very nice strawwork bags and sun-hats, jewellery and all kinds of woodcarving and pictures,' said Maria. 'It's where the tourists go to get something really Florentine. But you may prefer the San Lorenzo market; that has marvellous silks and leatherware at good prices.'

'I'd love to see both, if you'll come too and give me the right advice,' smiled Pauline.

The morning passed quickly, and Pauline was enthralled by everything she saw. After much debating and comparing of the two ancient markets' treasures, she finally decided on a framed reproduction of a nine-teenth-century view of Florence fromn the Boboli Gardens, painted by Corot. She also insisted on buying a silk scarf for Maria in recompense for her help, and could not resist a box of decorative writing paper of traditional Florentine design for herself, and a thick notebook for Nina, with a rainbow of gilded colours on the cover.

She then turned to her companion with an apologetic air.

'I wonder if I could ask you a favour, Maria?' she said casually. 'I want to walk up to Santa Maria Nuova, to enquire about a couple of patients who were admit-ted there last week after an accident. I don't really want to carry this picture around with me, so could I leave it at your apartment and collect it later?'

Maria hesitated just for a moment, and then said that she was sure it would be all right.

'Will it cause any inconvenience?' Pauline asked, noting the slight pause.

'No, Pauline, only—Annalisa's brother will be visiting her some time today, and Elena and I felt that we should keep out of the way, you understand? But if it is only to leave your picture, then surely it cannot be a problem, and they might have gone out for lunch anyway.'

She pulled a face and gave a pleading look as she added, 'And please, *please*, Pauline, remember that Annalisa does not know that it was I who wrote to the doctor. I do not want her to find out.'

Pauline gave her word that she would tell no tales,

and followed Maria along a wide street and across a square into a narrower street. Her heart pounded in apprehension of what she might encounter, and she wondered how she had ever had the nerve to make such a bold plan as this. Suppose Annalisa was furiously angry at her intrusion, and Niccolo blamed Maria for bringing her to his sister's apartment without permission? She would have to be very diplomatic indeed.

A narrow entrance between two buildings led to a high iron gate which Maria unlocked with a key from her bag. Pauline went through and found herself in a charming, sunny courtyard with intricate mosaic paving and a central cluster of shrubs in which three marble urns blazed with scarlet geraniums and begonias. An outside flight of steps ran diagonally up to a first floor balcony with graceful arches along its length, and two more storeys soared above, their casement windows opening on to smaller balconies festooned with flowers in hanging baskets and trailing from the wrought-iron balustrades. The thought came into Pauline's head that it was a perfect setting for *Romeo and Juliet*.

'Good heavens, Maria, is this the place where you live?' she marvelled. 'It's like a medieval palace!'

'It *is*,' replied Maria.

'The Palazzo Alessandra. It used to be a family home, but now the owner lets it out as apartments. Annalisa has the top floor, and shares it with Elena and me.'

'Isn't it—er—very expensive?' asked Pauline as she followed Maria up the stone steps to the first floor and through an archway leading to an inside staircase with gilded white banisters curving up to the second floor.

'Annalisa's brother pays her rent, and she charges us much less than the other tenants pay,' explained

MILLS & BOON

AN IMPORTANT MESSAGE FROM THE EDITORS OF MILLS & BOON

Dear Reader,

Because you've chosen to read one of our romance novels, we'd like to say "thank you"! And, as a **special** way to thank you, we've selected <u>four more</u> of the <u>books</u> you love so much, **and** a lovely necklace to send you absolutely <u>**FREE!**</u>

Please enjoy them with our compliments...

Tessa Shapcott Editor, Mills & Boon

P.S. And because we value our customers we've attached something extra inside...

EDITOR'S
FREE GIFT SEAL
THANK YOU

PEEL OFF SEAL AND PLACE INSIDE

HOW TO VALIDATE
YOUR
EDITOR'S FREE GIFT
"THANK YOU"

1. Peel off gift seal from front cover. Place it in space provided at right. This automatically entitles you to receive four free books and a lovely Austrian crystal necklace.

2. Send back this card and you'll get four specially selected Love on Call novels. These books have a cover price of £1.99 each, but they are yours to keep absolutely free.

3. There's no catch. You're under no obligation to buy anything. We charge nothing for your first shipment. And you don't have to make any minimum number of purchases - not even one!

4. The fact is thousands of readers enjoy receiving books by mail from Mills & Boon Reader Service. They like the convenience of home delivery and they like getting the best new novels at least a month before they're available in the shops. And, of course, postage and packing is completely FREE!

5. We hope that after receiving your free books you'll want to remain a subscriber. But the choice is yours - to continue or cancel, anytime at all! So why not take us up on our invitation, with no risk of any kind. You'll be glad you did!

6. Don't forget to detach your FREE BOOKMARK. And remember... just for validating your Editor's Free Gift Offer, we'll send you FIVE MORE gifts, *ABSOLUTELY FREE!*

NOT ACTUAL SIZE

You'll look like a million dollars when you wear this lovely necklace! Its cobra-link chain is a generous 18" long, and the multi-faceted Austrian crystal sparkles like a diamond!

THE EDITOR'S "THANK YOU" FREE GIFTS INCLUDE:

► Four Love on Call novels.
► A lovely Austrian crystal necklace.

PLACE
FREE GIFT
SEAL
HERE

1A6D

► DETACH BOOKMARK HERE ►

YES! I have placed my Editor's "thank you" seal in the space provided above. Please send me four free books and lovely necklace. I understand I am under no obligation to purchase any books, as explained on the back and on the opposite page.

BLOCK CAPITALS PLEASE

MS/MRS/MISS/MR

ADDRESS

POSTCODE

Thank you!

MAILING
PREFERENCE
SERVICE

© 1991 HARLEQUIN ENTERPRISES LTD.

Maria. 'We are all friends, you see.'

In other words, Niccolo subsidises your rents, sur-
mised Pauline, to ensure the right sort of company for
his sister.

With an outward calm that hid her inward turmoil,
she ascended a third staircase to the top floor and a
little hallway, from which an open door led into a
living-room, a *salotto*, from where upraised voices
could be heard. A man's and a woman's—pleading,
threatening, defying. Pauline could understand about
one in three of the furious torrent of words, but she
at once identified the man's voice. He sounded to be
at the very end of his patience and endurance.

'*O Dio mio*, they are having a row!' whispered
Maria. 'We had better leave your picture in the hall,
just inside the door.'

But Pauline saw her opportunity; it might never
come again.

'I want to speak to them, Maria. There is no need
for you to come in,' she muttered under her breath.
'And no need to wait for me.'

'But, Pauline, you don't know——' began Maria,
her eyes round with astonishment at this English girl
who was about to step in where angels feared to tread.
A Ghiberti quarrel was a formidable prospect.

'Goodbye, Maria,' insisted Pauline. 'And
thank you.'

The girl hurried away down the stairs, and Pauline
braced herself. It was now or never.

CHAPTER SIX

SHE sailed into the *salotto*, pleasantly businesslike.

'*Buongiorno, Niccolo e Annalisa.* I beg your pardon for intruding like this, but I heard you talking, and would like to offer my help,' she announced, in the best Italian she could muster, smiling in a friendly way at Annalisa and nodding in Niccolo's direction. It was the girl she needed to influence, and she tried to imagine that Annalisa was Nina, and to speak to her in the same way that she did to that pitiable girl.

The brother and sister were both so taken aback by her entrance that they broke off their arguing and just stared at the intruder in utter amazement. It gave Pauline time to take in Annalisa's woefully thin face and drawn features. Niccolo, too, looked exhausted, his black brows accentuating the lean, hard lines of his face. His jaw had dropped in mid-sentence as he was issuing an ultimatum to his sister.

'Paolina!'

The single word rose spontaneously to his lips, and he looked as shocked as if he had seen a ghost. Remembering her own bewilderment when he had appeared on the plane, Pauline could imagine how he felt, caught totally off-guard. She must use this fact to her advantage, she realised, and stay in control.

'I called to leave a picture here while I visit at the hospital,' she went on, 'and I could not help overhearing you.'

'Who the hell are you?' demanded Annalisa, finding

her voice and speaking in Italian. Pauline knew that everything depended upon her ability to win over this girl.

'My name is Pauline Stephens, and I am a friend of Maria,' she replied, also in Italian.

'And of my brother?' asked the girl, as sarcastically as she had spoken in the Boboli Gardens.

'We have worked together as doctor and nurse, yes, but nothing more. It is *you* I am interested in, Annalisa.'

Out of the corner of her eye she saw Niccolo open his mouth to speak, and then close it again as if he had no words left—as if his anxiety over his sister had drained him of all ideas. So much the better if he was now willing to give her a free hand, thought Pauline.

'Why should you be interested in *me*?' demanded Annalisa.

'Because I am a nurse and like working with young people who have problems,' Pauline answered matter-of-factly. 'You remind me of another friend of Maria's—Nina, a patient at the clinic where I work. She's very clever, but like you she's too thin! Though she's starting to improve—and so could you, Annalisa, if you'd come to the clinic for a while, say three weeks, and let me—let us help *you*, too.'

'Did my brother put you up to this?' asked the girl sharply.

'Certainly not. Dr Ghiberti has never been inside the Clinico Silverio, and I shall have to persuade him as well as you,' replied Pauline, avoiding Niccolo's eye.

'I doubt if you'll succeed. He says that your clinic's just for wealthy women who pretend that they're ill and pay to be fussed over,' replied Annalisa crushingly.

'And Maria has told me about this Nina. She sounds crazy!'

'I hope that Maria has also told you of the good results at the clinic, and the many successful treatments,' answered Pauline, sitting herself down in a comfortable armchair. 'Maria herself, for instance!'

Annalisa stared back at her, and all of a sudden she sat down too, or rather collapsed into a matching armchair. All the fight seemed to go out of her, and Pauline looked with real compassion upon a girl who was weary of struggling with ill-health.

Niccolo made a movement to go to his sister's side, but Pauline held up a warning hand and mouthed the word 'no.' He hesitated and then he, too, sat down and folded his arms. God only knew how or why this amazing girl had appeared at such a moment of crisis, he thought, but her air of authority seemed to be achieving more than all his rational arguments. Let her take over, then, and see what she could do!

For a few moments there was silence, giving Pauline a chance to look around the room. It had a beautifully carved wood ceiling, and a cool tiled floor in red, black and white with crimson rugs. A big hooded fireplace at one end had niches on each side for ornaments in marble, bronze and glass, and the furniture was all of superb quality and design.

She noticed an emblazoned gold 'G' above a long mirror hung on the wall opposite the fireplace. It was a gracious room, with a serenity that had withstood the changes of time and circumstance, and seemed to detach itself from the scene of disharmony now being played out. In a curious way Pauline drew strength from it, and she deliberately leaned back in the chair, allowing her tension to relax while she waited for

Annalisa to answer her last remark. When the girl eventually spoke, Pauline knew that she was halfway to gaining her objective.

'Maria says you live on raw vegetables and fruit at that clinic.'

'Not at all! Like Nina, you would eat whatever you like—chocolate, pastries, ice-cream—personally I can't resist Italian ice-cream. What are your favourite flavours?'

'And I wouldn't be forced to eat a lot of salad stuff?' asked Annalisa with a shudder, ignoring the question.

'No, you would not be forced to do anything at all,' Pauline assured her.

'Sounds boring.'

'I don't know what your special interests are, Annalisa, but I'm sure we'd find something to please you.'

'Like weaving silly little baskets, you mean?'

Pauline looked at her levelly. 'If you like making traditional straw baskets, that could be arranged. Nina prefers Renaissance literature and writes quite impressive verses herself. And we have a man whose oil paintings are so popular that he sells them to pay for his treatment. He can hardly keep up with the demand.'

She did not add that this particular patient had needed long and agonising therapy to wean him off the cocaine which had threatened to ruin his artistic career.

'I studied architecture for a short time at university,' said Annalisa, with a reminiscent gleam in her mournfully large eyes.

'Then what about studying it again with Sister Agnello?' asked Pauline, and just for a moment she caught Niccolo's eyes, now full of incredulous admiration. She gave him only the slightest of nods;

it was important to keep the upper hand.

'Did you say three weeks?' asked Annalisa.

'Yes, but it doesn't have to be three weeks exactly.
A little longer if you like being with us——'

'Or a little shorter if I don't!'

'Yes, of course. It's a hospital, not a prison,' said
Pauline lightly.

'Starting when?'

Pauline saw that she was almost there, but made a
point of concealing her triumph.

'Whenever you like. Dr and Signora Alberi will be
happy to see you at any time. What about Monday?
Talk it over with Dr Ghiberti and give it a try!'

She opened her handbag and took out a card.

'Here's the telephone number and a few details
about the clinic. You'll love the situation—it's in a
beautiful setting.'

Annalisa could not resist a last kick of defiance.

'I don't think Niccolo will be very keen for me to
go to that place—will you, Niccolo?' She turned and
looked at her brother with a malicious little smile.
'You've always said that private clinics are a money-
making racket, and no self-respecting doctor would be
seen dead in one!'

Niccolo did not answer, but drew a long breath and
slowly let it out again. Pauline suspected that he was
counting up to ten, or even twenty.

'Dr Ghiberti's entitled to his opinion,' she said
easily, keeping her eyes on the girl. 'And now you
must both excuse me as I want to visit at Santa Maria
Nuova. I shall look forward to hearing from you again,
Annalisa, OK?'

She got up from her chair and held out her hand,
first to Annalisa, who shook it limply with cold fingers,

and then to Niccolo, who held it between his own as
if he would have raised it to his lips. But she withdrew
it, much against her inclination. She lowered her eyes
to avoid looking into those dark depths; to give herself
away in front of Annalisa could undo all the good work
she had done.

'*Buongiorno!*' She smiled towards them both.

'*Buongiorno, Signorina Stephens, e molte grazie,*'
replied Niccolo, all traces of Ghiberti haughtiness overcome by sheer relief.

Still avoiding eye contact, Pauline walked out of the
apartment and descended the three flights of stairs,
trembling but triumphant. She had done it!

Enrico presented a sorry sight in the orthopaedic ward,
lying in his bed surmounted by a traction frame. His
mother sat at his side with her rosary beads in her
hand, and got up at once when she saw Pauline, smiling
and shaking her hand warmly.

The young man's eyes brightened, too.

'*La bella signorina inglese,*' he marvelled, his white
face still marked with fading bruises, and the line of
the scar livid from nose to jaw. He lay on his back
with his left leg encased in plaster from which metal
pins protruded, attached by double cords to a weight
hanging below the end of the bed. He seized the hand
that Pauline held out.

'The poor old lady went out of hospital after two
days,' he said in Italian. 'God forgive me, I might
have killed her. I have been a fool, but not any more,
signorina.'

His eyes filled with tears, and Pauline saw that the
shock of the accident had turned Enrico at a stroke
from a carefree boy into a man who would exercise

caution and consideration in the future. She smiled, and took a bar of fruit and nut chocolate out of her bag.

'You look a lot better than when I saw you last, Enrico. Just get back on your feet, and remember what you've said. We're all thankful that nothing worse happened—aren't we, *signora*?' she said, turning to his mother. That stout lady nodded tearfully, and on a sympathetic impulse Pauline leaned over the bed and kissed the pale young man gently on the forehead.

'God bless you, and good luck! I'm glad to see you getting better,' she whispered.

His answering smile ended in a wince as his scar moved, and his next words were very unexpected indeed.

'*Buongiorno*, Dr Ghiberti!'

Pauline froze, then slowly raised her head from bending over Enrico to see Niccolo standing on the opposite side of the bed, holding her picture under his arm. The *signora* greeted him with joy and for a few moments he could hardly get a word in edgeways, which gave Pauline a little time to compose herself.

'I was—er—just saying goodbye,' she said, flustered both by his unexpected appearance and at being found giving poor Enrico a consoling kiss. At least his mother had been looking on and approving!

At length they managed to make their farewells and leave the bedside; once out of the ward, Niccolo turned to her in some urgency.

'Forgive me for intruding on you, Pauline, but it is necessary that we talk, yes? Do you have to return to Fiesole straight away, or have you time to come for a coffee and maybe a pizza somewhere?'

'No—I mean, yes, of course—I am not in a hurry,' stumbled Pauline, finding that after the supreme effort she had made in Annalisa's apartment, reaction had set in and she was back to her usual dithering in this man's presence. Plus that infuriating tendency to blush! She did not realise how she appeared to him, prettily pink-cheeked and bright-eyed.

'Good! My car's in the hospital car park. If you will wait at the front entrance, I'll come and pick you up in two minutes,' he told her.

While she waited Pauline wondered what it was that he had to say to her. Had Annalisa changed her mind already? Or had he?

He drove expertly by various one-way systems in his privileged doctor's car, and crossed to the south bank, to the wide Piazza Santo Spirito.

'We can park here and walk down to the Borgo Antico—the old village,' he said. 'There are some good restaurants there, but the streets are too narrow for cars. Come, Paolina.'

There was an unfathomable look in his eyes as he guided her down a cramped cobbled street and into a small and intimate *trattoria*, where they were shown to a table for two in an alcove designed for lovers' meetings and private conversations.

At that afternoon hour the place was fairly empty, and when the waitress brought the menu Pauline chose a salad with creamy ricotta cheese and a wedge of delicious *focaccia*, the flat savoury bread made with olive oil. Niccolo asked for salami salad, and persuaded Pauline to take a glass of local wine. He seemed intent on attending to her every need and comfort, and she felt herself relaxing as she sipped the cool, fruity red wine.

Across the table she looked into his face, and she saw a variety of emotions depicted in his deeply shadowed eyes. His facial contours seemed leaner, and there were finely etched lines at the corners of his eyes and mouth that she had not noticed previously. Two vertical furrows between the long eyebrows had deepened into an almost habitual frown, reflecting a continuous anxiety, a conflict of allegiances. Pauline felt that she could imagine how this man might look in twenty years' time—still handsome in his fifties, but with the mobile features hardened into a sombre resignation that would take the hope from his eyes and quench his lively spirit. Her tender heart yearned over him as she waited for him to speak.

'What can I say, Paolina? You look at me so intently that I hope you can see the regret I feel for the way I have behaved.'

His voice was low and his tone unmistakably genuine. Pauline longed to reassure him.

'If you mean not telling me about Annalisa, I understand, Niccolo,' she said softly. 'It's natural that you want to keep family matters private. I'm sorry that I plagued you with questions about your return to Florence. It really was none of my business!'

'No, it is I who should apologise,' he insisted. 'We cannot keep our lives private, and why should we try to hide our circumstances from our friends? I should have known that you would learn the Ghiberti family history through the hospitals' grapevine—hah!' He gave a short, self-deprecating laugh. 'And I might have guessed that Maria would talk about her flatmate's problem!'

'Don't blame Maria, she means well,' said Pauline quickly. 'She told me herself that it was she who wrote to you, and I've promised not to tell Annalisa. And, after all, it's just as well that she *did*, isn't it?'

He sighed ruefully. 'Maybe—my sister plagues me every time I see her to name the interfering busybody! Poor Annalisa, that is the least of her problems. Oh, Paolina!' He closed his eyes briefly and shook his head. 'I have been at my wits' end over her. You have heard about the terrible loss we suffered four years ago?'

'Yes, Niccolo, and what can I possibly say? It must have been so dreadful for you both.' Her voice was very soft.

'It was, Paolina. Terrible. And if I had only caught the train home, or taken a taxi, instead of telephoning my father to come and pick me up at the airport—*O mio Dio*! The weather was very bad—wet and stormy—and it was I, Paolina, who brought my father and mother out to their deaths on the *autostrada* that night. Yes, I am haunted for life by that knowledge, and poor Annalisa is also damaged because of my selfishness and thoughtlessness. She was so adored by her father—oh, I cannot tell you what she suffered——'

Pauline stared in horror as his voice broke at the recollection of the tragedy, and she swiftly put out her hand and laid it firmly over his on the table.

'Nonsense, Niccolo,' she said, quietly but with authority. 'You were not to know what would happen. It was a tragic accident such as could happen at any time—a chance, a stroke of misfortune. Yes, I can see that it has had a bad effect on Annalisa, but other people have suffered losses and had to survive. She can't go all through her life blaming the accident for her health problems, and you mustn't carry a lifelong burden, either, Niccolo. Look, I don't want to sound harsh, but it's time Annalisa grew up, and at the Clinico Silverio she'll be helped to do just that.'

'I wish I could be as sure, Paolina. God knows, I've tried to get her to stand on her own feet and help herself. It was partly because she accused me of always fussing over her and treating her as a child that I applied to the exchange scheme for the year in Beltonshaw.'

Pauline raised her eybrows, remembering Stefano's words.

'Now she accuses me of trying to interfere in her life,' he went on, 'but she does not see that it is because I love her and want to take the place of the dear father she lost. God knows that it was my loss, too—I dearly loved them both—but I have had my work to help me to overcome the sorrow and carry on living. Poor Annalisa cannot hold down a job, no matter how promising it seems at first—she always regresses back to this accursed anorexia. Oh, *God*!'

To her infinite pity Pauline saw raw pain in his eyes, and as he blinked there was moisture on his black lashes.

'Forgive me, Paolina. I should not trouble you with all this. But I can never turn my back on her—you do understand that, yes?'

'Of course, Niccolo. I understand—I do, truly,' she told him as tears of shared sadness welled up in her own eyes. She kept her hand over his in the privacy of the alcove as she went on, 'But now there is a ray of hope for her and you. I'm convinced that if anything can sort her out, it's the therapy and counselling team of the Clinico Silverio.'

'Dear Paolina! Heaven knows why you should take such trouble over a girl who has been so—so impolite to you,' he said with a baffled air.

How could he know that it was all for love of

him—this Florentine doctor who had appeared in her life scarcely six weeks ago and overturned it?

'I'm a nurse, remember,' she said lightly, removing her hand from his as the waitress served their salads. 'To me Annalisa is just another patient in need of care. Nina can be every bit as trying!' She laughed and rolled up her eyes in mock exasperation.

'Surely not worse than poor Annalisa!'

'I'll reserve judgement on that one,' she replied. 'It will be interesting to see what they make of each other. I say, this salad is delicious—I hadn't realised how hungry I was.'

'Did you not have lunch?' he asked in surprise.

'Er—no. I spent the morning shopping with Maria, and we just had a coffee-break,' she answered, not adding that the prospect of tackling Annalisa had hung over her head all the morning and taken away her appetite. But now all that was successfully behind her, and she was having lunch with a grateful Niccolo. She bit into the *focaccia* with relish, and allowed herself a generous helping of salad.

He insisted on driving her back to the Clinico Silverio.

'I shall need to see Riccardo anyway,' he pointed out a little reluctantly. 'We did our medical training together, but we haven't been close in recent years, and I've never met his wife—your friend.'

Pauline realised that this meeting would involve a degree of climb-down on Niccolo's part, and assured him that Jenny would be pleased to meet him, though she, too, felt some embarrassment at the thought of Jenny's reaction on seeing Niccolo so soon after their conversation about the Ghibertis and her own confession about her feelings for him. Much as she enjoyed

the drive at his side in the afternoon sunshine, she half
dreaded the moment of arrival.

She need not have worried. Jenny was discreetly
polite, pretending not even to know about Annalisa,
and when Niccolo asked if he might have a private
word with Dr Alberi, Riccardo was all smiles and excla-
mations of delight on seeing his former friend and
fellow student again.

'It has been too long, Niccolo! Come and take a
glass of wine in the study, and we'll talk about the
times when we were young!' he invited, and, with arms
flung around each other's shoulders, the two thirty-
one-year-old doctors went off together, chuckling over
memories of each other's youthful escapades.

Jenny then beckoned Pauline into her office off the
reception area, and closed the door.

'So, Pauline, your mission was successful, I gather?'

'Yes! Isn't it wonderful, Jenny—I've *done* it!'
crowed Pauline, spinning round on one foot. 'Annalisa
will be coming to join the family on Monday. It's just
so good of you and Riccardo, and I'm *sure* you'll sort
her out here!'

'We'll certainly try, love. We'll do our best and give
her all we've got,' promised Jenny. 'But listen, Pauline,
you've got another problem, I'm afraid.'

'Oh? What's that?' asked Pauline, alarmed by
Jenny's grave expression.

'Stefano Sandrini has been on the phone, asking for
you urgently. Things don't sound too good at Vernio,
Pauline. In fact, Joanna's completely flipped her lid,
by his description.'

'Oh, *no!*' cried Pauline in dismay. 'And I wasn't
even here to take the call—poor Stefano! And Joanna
and my poor little Toni—I *knew* I should have

gone to Vernio with them. Oh, what shall I *do*?' she
wailed.

Jenny was sympathetic but firm. 'Well, for a start
you're on the staff here now, and under contract to
Riccardo, love. We can't spare you for anything less
than a personal family crisis. I had to tell Signor
Sandrini that.'

'Oh, *no*!' repeated Pauline, sitting down and putting
her head in her hands. If only she could cut herself
in half!

'And besides, you'll want to be here for Annalisa,
won't you?' added Jenny significantly, knowing that
this was of paramount importance to Pauline, who
nodded, not looking up. She could see no way out of
this latest dilemma.

'Cheer up, love,' said Jenny kindly. 'Riccardo and
I know how badly you must feel about the Sandrinis,
and we've devised a plan that we think will be for the
best all round.'

Pauline looked up quickly. 'What do you
mean, Jenny?'

'Riccardo had a word with the poor man, and recommended that he bring Joanna here for rest and
assessment by Dr Luongo.'

'Oh, *bless* you!' Pauline exclaimed thankfully. 'And
did Stefano agree?'

'Yes, he wanted to bundle her into the car then
and there, but Riccardo advised waiting till tomorrow.
Their own doctor has prescribed a sedative, and she's
to take one tonight and one again tomorrow before
the journey. That will give Stefano's mother time to
pack a suitcase for her—and the baby, of course. He'll
be admitted with his mother, as Dr Luongo likes to
maintain the relationship in cases like this. So you'll

have plenty of work on your hands next week, Pauline, with Annalisa and Joanna, not to mention a couple of admissions to the surgical suite today for op on Monday.'

'That's fine, Jenny. I don't mind hard work, and I'll gladly spend my off-duty time next week with Joanna and Annalisa,' answered Pauline without hesitation. 'I just can't thank you enough, you and Riccardo!'

She went over to her friend and hugged her gratefully.

'And how is my darling Toni, did Stefano say?' she asked, remembering the many hours she had spent assisting that unpredictable little baby to breast-feed.

'Apparently he cries a lot—not surprisingly, as the tension must affect him,' sighed Jenny. 'He'll be taken to a separate room at night, and fed by the night staff——'

'He'll come to *my* room,' said Pauline. '*I'll* look after him at night, poor little fellow. I owe it to him.'

'My dear Pauline, you can't do that!' objected Jenny. 'No off-duty time during the day, and an unhappy baby all night——'

'I don't want him to be cared for by busy nurses at night, Jenny. He comes to *me*, right?'

Jenny saw that she was adamant, and that to argue the point would be wasting her breath.

When Niccolo emerged from Riccardo's study, he was immediately concerned to see Pauline's worried face, and drew her aside to ask what the matter was. When he heard about the Sandrinis' problems, he looked grave.

'Poor Signora Sandrini! It is as you feared, Paolina,' he murmured, shaking his head.

'I knew in my heart that I should have gone to Vernio,' she admitted with a sigh. 'And you said so, too, Niccolo.'

'You must not reproach yourself now, *cara mia*. It is perhaps best that the *signora* comes here. It would be a great anxiety for you, coping alone with a serious postnatal depression. And if you had gone to Vernio. . .'

He looked down at her with a sudden longing to cradle her in his arms and wipe away the tears of regret shining on her lashes. Instead he tucked her right arm under his left, and led her along the cloistered walk that circled the courtyard. When they reached the archway that led out of the grounds they passed under it and continued to walk along the outside of the wall, turning left round a corner that hid them from view of the approach road. They were alone, with the sun-warmed stone wall on one side and a green expanse around them, leading to wooded hills to the north-west. A cluster of thickly flowering gorse grew close up to the wall at one point, leaving only a narrow stony path for them to pass along. Niccolo went first, and helped her through into a sheltered semi-circle of grass-grown paving.

'You look tired, Paolina. It has been a long day for you, yes?' His voice was low and tender, and she realised how utterly weary she was. Without thinking, she instinctively let her head rest against him; it fitted perfectly into the hollow below his left shoulder—a natural and right place for her head to be, or so it felt to her.

'Paolina——' he began, and encircled her body in the curve of his arm.

'Yes? What is it, Niccolo?' she asked softly, thinking

that this was the nearest to heaven that she could imagine.

'Only that you have been so sweet, so forgiving towards me and to my sister, little Paolina—and I want to tell you——'

She opened her mouth to speak, but he gently placed his forefinger over her lips.

'Shh, *cara mia*, let me say what I must say. It is precisely because you are so kind that I worry about you. I have doubts that Annalisa will ever be really well, and to speak the truth, I do not hope for too much. She is a difficult girl, I know, and has not been right since our great loss, as I said before. It may be that she will have to bear this burden for life, and what I want to say is that you must not be too disappointed, or, worse still, blame yourself if she—if she cannot be cured here.'

His voice had lowered, and the last sentence was barely audible. As she took in what he was saying, his warning her of possible failure and exonerating her in advance, her heart overflowed with the love she felt for him, and her pity for the sorrow that over-shadowed his life.

'Niccolo—oh, Niccolo!'

It was just a whisper, but he tightened his hold; her arms strayed up around his neck and she moved her head until her face was buried against his shoulder. The warmth, the wholesome maleness of him enveloped her as his arms closed around her waist, and his dark head lowered until it rested upon hers. She heard the thud of his heartbeat through his clothes, and also the sound of him whispering something in Italian; his lips were at her ear, on her hair, touching her cheek. . . She felt his clean skin against her face, the very slight roughness of a dark-haired man who had not shaved since morning. He brimmed with vitality; it flowed out from him like an electric charge.

'*Dolce, dolce—o, Paolina, dolcezza!*'

And then the world stood still for her as his kiss claimed her lips, and sweetly, softly, her mouth opened to him like a flower. The cloudless blue sky above them, the golden gorse, the pale, smooth stone of the wall against which they leaned—all were part of an enchanted moment in the May afternoon turning into evening.

To Niccolo her slender body was like a priceless marble statue coming to life in his embrace—warm, living flesh, fragrant and inviting. He was intoxicated by her.

'Paolina. . .'

Now she felt the powerful masculinity of him, the firm muscle beneath his shirt, the hardness of his thighs; she seemed to melt against him, her soft breasts aching for his touch. As if he understood that silent longing, he withdrew his hands from her waist and laid the palms against her blouse, cupping each breast with a kind of worship. Turning her round so that her back was against the wall, he began to undo her buttons; she felt his hands slide in under the thin material and unfasten the bra-hook at her back. She sighed wordlessly, and a tremor ran through her whole frame.

'Sweet, sweet—my beautiful Paolina,' he muttered thickly, bending his head further to kiss her neck and throat; she reached up to kiss his left ear, his forehead, his nose—until her breath was taken away by a more urgent pressure of his lips upon hers. She felt his teeth, his tongue, and her knees went weak as a great wave of desire swept over her. She swayed against him,

wanting only to be all-in-all to him, with no thought
for yesterday or tomorrow.

'*Niccolo*!'

It was the sound of the longing in her voice, the
sight of the passion in her swimming blue-grey eyes that
both tempted and restrained Niccolo at that moment of
decision. Though he wanted her with every fibre of
his being, the weight of life and experience—especially
during the past four years—had impressed care and
caution upon him. Duty and commitment also exer-
cised their powerful influence to pull him back from
the course which his heart and mind and manhood so
cried out for.

Within his head the man responded with a glad yes
to her sweetness, but the doctor more decisively said
no; this was no time to take advantage of the English
nurse who had been so kind to him in every way. And
with possible consequences for which he was not yet
prepared. . .

'No, Paolina. Paolina, no. *No*.' It had to be said,
but the words were wrenched out of him with an almost
physical pain.

'Niccolo,' she murmured again, drawing his head
down to the softly curving breasts held out to him.

'No, *cara mia*, no. This is not the time.' The words
were a groan as he drew back from the brink, feeling
that only God knew the effort it had cost him.

It seemed to Pauline as if she swam down through
the shimmering air to land once more upon the earth.
The *earth*—the real world that held sadness and illness,
the demands of work, of family, of friends, of everyday
life. She closed her eyes and passively let him rearrange
her clothes, felt his fingers with infinite gentleness
refastening her bra and buttoning her shirt. He kissed

her lovingly on the forehead and drew her arm through
his as they began to walk slowly back along the way
they had come, under the archway and into the
courtyard.

Jenny and Riccardo sat talking near the entrance to
the clinic, and waved to them as they reappeared.

'And about time, too!' Jenny called gaily. 'We were
just about to send a search-party!'

'Do not grudge them a little romantic walking and
talking, Jenny,' pleaded her husband with a smile.
'With Signora Sandrini and the baby coming tomorrow,
and Signorina Ghiberti on Monday, there will be little
time soon for lovers to walk and talk, no?'

CHAPTER SEVEN

BEFORE she got into bed that night, Pauline knelt on the bench seat below her window and gazed towards the Tuscan hills outlined in the moonlight. The memory of Niccolo's kisses burned upon her skin; she still felt the touch of the firm hands that had caressed her, arousing a response that she had not been able to hide. She closed her eyes and sighed in recollection of that overwhelming masculinity that had so melted and moved her. And yet he had withdrawn from her, gently and lovingly it was true, but with a definite refusal to commit himself further. . .

Had she been too eager, too easy in her response? She felt her lack of sophistication in these matters, recalling with regret the tumultuous lovemaking of Giorgio, the ecstasy and then the heartbreak when he had lost interest after the holiday. *He* had shown no caution, and she had later bitterly regretted her eager consent.

Niccolo had said no to her eagerness—and yet there was no doubt at all that he had found her desirable, and that, combined with his gratitude for her offer of help with Annalisa, led her to conclude that he must have acted on impulse and then changed his mind. She supposed that his anxiety over his sister left no room in his life to engage in a serious love affair.

Yet how could she *not* have responded, caring for him as she did? Whatever his feelings for her, Pauline knew that she was deeply in love with Niccolo Ghiberti.

*　　*　　*

On Sunday morning she went to the surgical suite early, intending to get well ahead with her work before the Sandrinis arrived. A large, overweight and self-indulgent woman in her forties had been admitted for a cholecystectomy—removal of gall-bladder—on Monday morning, and a banker's wife was in for a hysterectomy.

Pauline secretly thought both women typical of the kind described by Niccolo in his comments on small private hospitals like this, but she reminded herself that the very high fees their husbands were paying would benefit other patients. She explained to them the preparations that would be made for surgery, and the large lady's face fell at hearing that there would be no breakfast on Monday, only an early cup of tea. Neither of them was entranced by the thought of a suppository, and both had an aversion to needles, so Pauline had to explain that the small injection of a sedative one hour prior to going to the theatre was well worth the brief prick involved.

'I shan't sleep a wink all night, thinking about you coming to me with that horrible syringe,' grumbled the oversized lady, wrapping an exquisite Indian shawl over her billowing silk nightie, and popping a chocolate into her mouth. 'Especially if I'm also to be deprived of my breakfast!'

'You'll be fine, don't worry, *signora*,' Pauline assured her brightly, thankful that a new Australian staff nurse was due to start work the next day in the surgical suite, as there would be some very heavy lifting to do.

But even Pauline's determined smile wavered when she saw Joanna Sandrini. A friend of Stefano's had driven the car from Vernio, so that Stefano could keep a close watch on his wife. His mother, a worried-looking, grey-haired woman, got out of the car clasping a howling Toni, and Joanna was helped out of the back seat where she had dozed on and off during the journey. She looked as if she had lost all interest in her appearance, her hair was unbrushed and her complexion muddy.

'Joanna! Oh, Joanna, *dear*!' cried Pauline, running to greet her with out-stretched arms.

But there was no answering smile; Joanna turned two lustreless eyes on her, and then looked away.

'*Joanna*!' Pauline took hold of her arm, but it was angrily shrugged off. 'I thought you were my friend, but you left me when I most needed you,' came the accusation. 'You didn't care what happened to me, and I don't care for *you*—not any more!'

Pauline stared in consternation at this changed person, feeling as if she had been slapped in the face.

'Please, Signorina Pauline, do not take notice. She is just the same to me,' said Stefano, wearily picking up his wife's suitcase. 'My Giovanna does not believe that we all love and care for——'

'Yes, go on and tell her lies about me! Discuss me with her, like you discuss me with your precious mother—don't think I don't know!' Joanna burst into angry tears, and Jenny hastily intervened, taking her by the arm and leading her into the clinic, while gesturing to Pauline to take Stefano and his mother with the baby to Dr Luongo's office.

While they waited there for the psychiatrist to arrive, Pauline heard Stefano's sad story.

'She sits and says nothing for hours, and then she bursts out into temper and cries till she has no tears left,' he told her. 'I try every way to reason with her, to console her, and——' his voice shook, and there were tears in his big brown eyes '—and if I try to make love to her, she looks at me as a stranger, and calls me bad names!'

The tears spilled down his plump cheeks as he went on, 'My mother and I, we dare not leave her alone with little Toni. I cannot continue to run my business while things are like this at home. *O mio Dio!*'

Pauline was deeply moved with pity for them all, and tried to reassure the distraught husband that his wife could be cured of her tragic disorder.

'But she listen to nobody!' retorted his mother. 'She no look after my son or his child or his home. Is completely mad!'

Pauline sighed and held out her arms to take Toni, who nestled against her, making little whimpering sounds. She kissed his soft cheek and stroked his head as she asked about his feeding.

'Sometimes she feed him, sometimes not,' replied Stefano helplessly. 'My mother gives him bottles. The nursemaid left because my Giovanna screamed at her and called her a——'

'Listen to me, both of you,' Pauline said firmly. 'Your Giovanna is ill, due to hormone imbalance, and the important thing to remember is that it is nobody's fault. Nobody is to blame. You have done your best, both of you, and now Dr Luongo will take over and help her to get well.'

At that moment Riccardo entered with Violetta Luongo, and Pauline left them, taking Toni to a room that had been prepared as a nursery for him.

That afternoon Violetta, a pretty woman in her late thirties with bright, bird-like eyes, spoke seriously to Pauline.

'I'm rather worried about her, Sister. She could have long-term puerperal psychosis. I would prefer you to stay away from her for the time being, and I have asked her husband not to visit before Wednesday. Mrs Alberi has arranged for a special nurse to remain with her at all times, and she is to be sedated for twenty-four hours, starting now. During this time the baby will be cared for in a separate room, and he is to be entirely bottle-fed on formula milk.'

Pauline nodded unhappily, making up her mind to spend as much time as possible with Toni, preparing his feeds and supplying the loving care that his mother was unable to give him at present.

'And after twenty-four hours of sedation, I will review her and decide what anti-depressant drugs to try,' went on Violetta.

'Do you think she'll need something like tryptozol or surmontal?' asked Pauline, naming drugs commonly used in psychiatry.

'I don't think so,' replied the doctor. 'Postnatal depression should not necessarily be treated in the same way as other types. I'm going to start her straight away on daily injections of progesterone, and I might try her on some new anti-depressants, which have been found to be effective in clinical trials—and they don't cause tiredness like the ones you've mentioned. If she continues to be seriously disturbed, I'll have to give largactil, but I need to monitor her carefully. We'll see how she reacts to a good long sleep!'

Pauline's heart ached when she said goodbye to Stefano.

'Don't give way to despair, and remember that Jo—Giovanna is in good hands,' she told him and his mother.

'Yes, Pauline—and I know that my son is in safe hands with *you*,' he answered with emotion. He kissed her cheek before getting into the car.

'*Arrivederci, cara Pauline*!'

That night in her room Pauline gave Toni his last feed of the day and held him close against her shoulder. He could now hold up his head on his flower-stalk neck, and as she smiled into his big dark eyes, so like his father's, his mouth curved up into a lovely smile that brightened his little round face.

'Oh, Toni, you little darling,' she whispered, holding his face to hers. 'Your poor mummy *must* get better for you and Daddy—she really and truly *must*!'

Monday morning brought a letter from Pauline's mother, with an early wedding invitation. Helen Stephens' marriage to Dr Graham Stafford was to take place on September the second at St Antony's Church, Beltonshaw, and she naturally wanted both her daughters to be there.

When Pauline read it at the breakfast table, her heart sank. Jenny's baby was expected in the first week of September, and not only would Pauline be needed at the clinic more than ever before, but she had as good as promised her friend to be present at the birth. To stay away from her mother's wedding would look like disapproval, but her good friends also depended on her. She decided to delay making a decision for the time being. At present there were so many other things on her mind—not the least of which was the thought of seeing Niccolo again when he arrived with Annalisa.

On duty in the surgical suite, she prepared her two ladies for theatre and met the big, blonde Australian staff nurse, Heather Hulland, who was to replace Kitty O'Hare. Two different surgeons were coming to perform the operations, and Pauline hid her nervousness under a determination to acquaint herself speedily with their methods of working.

Apart from a minor misunderstanding about which instrument was needed at one point during the cholecystectomy, the morning passed without mishap, and both surgeons appeared satisfied with the new sister's theatre technique. She heaved a sigh of relief, thinking of her frantic scrabble among her instruments to find the curved gall-bladder forceps which she knew under another name.

'You were pretty cute, Pauline,' grinned Heather, who had noted the moment of panic. 'Just as well our fat lady was mercifully oblivious at the time!'

When the two patients were back in their rooms and recovering from their anaesthetics, Pauline went straight to Toni's nursery to check on his feeds, for which she had made out a daily chart. His room, like Joanna's, opened on to a glass-covered passage overlooking a shrubbery. When she heard approaching footsteps, and the sound of Niccolo's voice, she held her breath and guessed that Riccardo must be showing the Ghibertis to Annalisa's room.

They passed by the door without seeing her, and were continuing on their way when there was a sudden disturbance. Joanna Sandrini, awaking from her long sleep, also heard Niccolo's deep tones, and before her special nurse could stop her she leapt from her bed and ran out into the passageway, dressed only in a short nightie. Flinging herself on the startled Niccolo, she threw her arms around his neck and sobbed with relief.

'*Dr Ghiberti*! Oh, Dr Ghiberti, thank God you're here—now at last I shall be easy in my mind!' she cried hysterically.

As soon as Niccolo realised who she was, he responded with gentle tact, unwinding her arms from his neck and holding both her hands in his.

'Signora Sandrini, you must return to your room, my dear,' said Riccardo, hastily suppressing his amusement. 'Dr Ghiberti is busy!'

'Oh, don't leave me, Doctor!' implored Joanna. 'You're the only one I can trust—I feel better just to know that you're near me!'

Pauline peeped from the doorway as Niccolo led Joanna back to her room, and with the nurse's assistance got her into the bed. He spent a few moments explaining that he had another patient to attend to, but would call back to see her later.

'Promise, Dr Ghiberti?' Pauline heard Joanna ask with childlike trust.

'Promise, *signora*. Only you'll have to be good and do what they tell you here, so that you can get better for your husband and little Toni,' he said kindly.

'I'll get better for *you*, Doctor,' came Joanna's reply as he released himself from her and returned to his sister.

'So *that's* what you get up to, Niccolo!' Pauline heard Annalisa say. 'How many more females are waiting to hang around your neck?'

Riccardo made some light-hearted remark, and the trio walked on. Pauline hardly knew what to think. In Joanna's seriously disturbed state it was important that she should not be upset, and Niccolo had been careful not to humiliate her by appearing to reject her. Even so, Pauline felt even sorrier for Stefano.

*   *   *

Annalisa was quickly initiated into a course of therapy which included daily counselling, a dietary programme and lessons in drawing and sketching, which was her choice of occupation. A blood count revealed an iron-deficiency anaemia, and she was prescribed iron and vitamin supplements. Her room was next to Nina's, and although the two girls were mutually suspicious at first, they discovered common ground.

Annalisa also seemed to get on with the psychiatric patients—the addicts whose weaknesses and failures had brought them to the point of desperation and a last tremendous effort to break free from the habits that had taken over their lives. It gave Annalisa a certain superiority—a welcome change from being pitied by her friends and scolded by her brother. She was evasive towards Pauline, however, who heard her mutter a remark in Italian that could have been translated as 'prying English bitch'. Pauline ignored it, but Jenny, who also heard, was very annoyed.

'You don't have to take that sort of talk, Pauline. I shall speak to her and tell her that we don't allow abusive language from anybody here.'

'No, Jenny, please leave her to me,' begged Pauline. 'I'm willing to put up with any amount of abuse if we can only get through to her, and find out what's really the matter.'

'Just because she's Niccolo's sister?' asked Jenny, unconvinced.

'You could say that, I suppose—please, Jenny, for my sake, don't reprimand her!'

'All right, then,' replied Jenny reluctantly. 'But she'd better not speak of any other members of staff like that. All I can say is, what some women will go through in the name of love!'

Pauline supposed that the girl had guessed her feelings for Niccolo, and suspected a conspiracy between
them—whereas in fact Pauline had not even spoken
to him since that magical Saturday evening.

On Wednesday at lunchtime Pauline and Heather
were sitting in the dining-room at a large table with a
group that included Violetta Luongo, Sister Agnello,
Nina, Annalisa, a young man who was being de-toxed
from heroin and the artist who was almost an ex-
cocaine addict.

Conversation flowed quite easily, and Pauline
noticed that Annalisa was obviously enjoying a portion
of steamed fish in white sauce. Heather was saying
something in her broad New South Wales twang, but
Pauline did not hear her, because all her attention was
focused on the couple who had just come into the
dining-room: Niccolo Ghiberti and a pale but
composed Joanna Sandrini. He led her to a table for
two where they were served with chicken salad.

Dr Luongo left her table and went to sit with the
couple for a while, exchanging a few remarks before
returning to the group. Nina and Annalisa were actually giggling together over some joke, and Pauline
wondered grimly if it was about Niccolo and his companion. Joanna certainly looked better than on the
day of her arrival, so the new drugs must be doing
her good.

Or could it have been Niccolo who had effected the
improvement?

'That's the third time I've asked if you want any
dessert, Pauline,' complained Heather good-naturedly.
'You seem to be a little out of it, sweetie.'

'Oh, I'm sorry, Heather. No, thanks,' answered
Pauline, knowing that the words were only too true;

she *was* feeling 'a little out of it'. Joanna's rejection of her was very upsetting, and she didn't seem to be needed by Annalisa or her brother. Very well, she would spend her afternoon off taking Toni out in the sunshine and relaxing under a parasol in the shrubbery with a historical novel.

She had forgotten about the attraction that a young baby held for women of all ages.

'*Guarda che bambino bello*, Annalisa!'

'*Si, è bellissimo!*'

Pauline was roused from a daydream by Nina and Annalisa bending over the baby and coaxing smiles from him.

'Do let me pick him up, Pauline!' begged Nina.

There was something very touching in the sight of the two thin, gaunt girls gazing down on the chubby six-week-old baby boy, who was now vocally demanding his next feed. Pauline lifted him out of the buggy, and went indoors to check his nappy and fetch the bottle she had prepared.

'Now, Nina, do you want to feed him?' she asked on her return. A clean and sweet-smelling Toni was carefully placed in Nina's eager arms as she sat on a padded garden chair. Pauline tucked a bib under the baby's chin, and all three of them laughed at the way he grabbed the teat and wolfed down half the milk within two minutes. Nina smiled radiantly for the first time since Pauline had known her.

'And his mother is that wild creature who hangs around my brother?' asked Annalisa scornfully.

Pauline frowned. 'Signora Sandrini is ill, and we must feel sorry for her,' she said coldly, and at that very moment she saw Niccolo and Joanna walking along the covered passageway. She was smiling up at him, and in response to something he said she let her head lie for a moment on his shoulder. Annalisa followed Pauline's eyes and saw them too; she gave a malicious little smile.

'So, Pauline, women who fall in love with doctors must be prepared for rivals among his lady patients, yes?'

'Oh, don't be *silly*!' Pauline snapped. 'The *signora* is nothing more to Dr Ghiberti than a sad, sick lady who needs a little understanding.'

But out of the corner of her eye she watched as Niccolo took his leave of Joanna, who put out her hands as if imploring him to stay. He shook his head, whispered something to her, patted her shoulder and, turning on his heel, he walked towards them, smiling.

Annalisa was distinctly cool. 'So you've managed to tear yourself away at last, Niccolo. *We*, as you see, are caring for her baby.'

'You seemed to be enjoying your lunch and the company so much, I did not like to intrude,' he replied lightly, then turned to Pauline with a much graver expression.

'Poor Signora Sandrini is very disturbed, yes? I hope that she is never left alone.'

'Of course she isn't,' replied Pauline a trifle impatiently. 'She has a special nurse who stays with her at all times.'

'Except when she's smooching around with some know-all doctor who's supposed to be visiting his sister,' added Annalisa, and for once Pauline felt that this tiresome girl had a point.

'All right, Annalisa, introduce me to your friend and tell me about life at the Clinico Silverio.' He smiled, with a sidelong glance at Pauline.

'Well, I suppose it is not *too* bad here,' conceded his sister. 'I mean, it could be worse—do you not think so, Nina?'

Coming from Annalisa, this was praise of a high order, and the next half-hour passed pleasantly enough, with Toni providing a happy focal point as she and Niccolo encouraged the girls to talk about whatever interested them. Nina was more forthcoming than Pauline had ever known her to be, but Annalisa managed to conceal her real thoughts under a sarcastic wit that irritated her brother and made Pauline wonder what this girl had to hide.

At four o'clock Dr Luongo came to take Toni from them.

'The *signora* is asking to see her baby,' she said with satisfaction. 'Her husband is coming to visit, and it will be nice for the three of them to be together for a little while. You have been good for her, Dr Ghiberti—she is beginning to respond to medication.'

With Toni gone, and the two girls having wandered off to relax beside the pool, Pauline was left alone with Niccolo and found herself rather at a loss for words, even though she had longed for this moment. Somehow the problems of the patients loomed between them.

'Paolina——' he began, and she realised that he too felt a certain awkwardness. 'I've got the rest of the day free, and I would like to take you out to dinner. There's a place near the Ponte Vecchio. . .'

Pauline hesitated. 'I'm due back on duty at half-past four,' she said, glancing at her watch, 'and I won't get off before eight-thirty—and I have Toni with me at night, so I couldn't stay out very long.' Far from being over-eager this time, she sounded definitely dubious, and Niccolo's disappointment was plain.

'Oh, I see. What about a meal in Fiesole? That's not far. And I *do* want to talk to you, Paolina,' he added, making it impossible for her to refuse.

'All right, Niccolo,' she said with sudden decision. 'And I'd be glad to talk, too. I'll leave a message with the night staff to look after Toni until I return. And now I really must get changed for the evening shift.'

'Good! I'll call for you at around eight on eight-thirty, and wait till you're ready,' he said, and in the warmth of his smile Pauline felt her spirits rising again. It was ridiculous to let herself become depressed by unhappy patients' problems, she told herself.

Or to resent their demands on her own patience and forbearance.

She and Heather were kept busy with their post-ops that evening. At eight o'clock she grabbed a quick cup of coffee and took it into the office where she started writing up the daily report cards and observation charts.

'Hey, Pauline! There's a bloke here asking to see you—sounds kinda urgent,' Heather called out to her. Pauline looked up, expecting to see an anxious relative—or had Niccolo arrived already?

But the agitated man who rushed into her office was Stefano Sandrini.

'It is no good, Pauline, I cannot stand by and see my wife give herself to another man!' he shouted. 'No man in his right mind would allow it!'

'Shh, calm yourself, Stefano, please, and sit down,' she ordered, afraid of the effect of such a disturbance on the patients in the suite. She closed the office door.

'All right, tell me all about it—slowly and quietly.'

'My Giovanna, she turns away from me, she insults my mother, she does not know how she feels about our baby—she talks only of this Ghiberti!'

Pauline felt a chill over her heart, a bleak fellow feeling with this spurned husband. She took his hand and he seized hers, wringing it between his own.

'She can't help it, Stefano, she's not herself——'

'Damned right, Pauline, she is *not* herself—not the lovely Giovanna I fall in love with and marry. Not this woman who runs after another man and then tells me that *I* have deserted *her*!'

Somehow Pauline managed to quieten him and persuade him to wait until his wife's anti-depressant medication had really had a chance to work. She assured him with as much conviction as she could muster that Dr Ghiberti had no ulterior motive towards her, but was merely humouring her disordered fantasies about himself.

'Believe me, Stefano, I *do* know how you feel,' she told him earnestly. 'But you *must* be patient and give her time.'

'And how long must I be parted from my Antonio, my little boy?' he asked sadly. 'She says she is no more his mother now because she does not feed him, no?'

Pauline closed her eyes. What a nightmare this was for the Sandrinis! And how long would it take for Joanna to wake from it to health and sanity again?

'Everything will be all right in the end, Stefano, you'll see.'

'You are kind, Pauline, but my world has collapsed around me.'

He looked so lost that she instinctively put out her

arms to comfort him. They hugged each other, the innocent embrace of friends.

'Oh, Pauline, you are an angel,' he whispered, and, enveloping her in his sturdy arms, the unhappy man buried his face against her neck and stifled a choking sob of despair.

And that was the scene that greeted Ghiberti when he came to the office. Getting no reply to his knock, he opened the door to see if the room was occupied. Pauline stared at him over the top of Stefano's shoulder. His black eyebrows shot up, but her blue-grey eyes blazed with an anger he had not seen before as she gestured furiously for him not to speak. The last thing she wanted was for the distressed and jealous Stefano to see him now.

'What——' began Niccolo, but Pauline cut him short.

'Will you please leave and close the door?' she requested. 'Can't you see I'm busy?'

For a moment Ghiberti stared in baffled defiance, clearly displeased to see her in such close proximity to a man she was presumably reassuring or advising in some way. He did not register the broad back as belonging to Joanna's husband, whom he had met only briefly in the Boboli Gardens.

'I asked you to kindly close the door and leave us,' Pauline repeated, waving him away with her hands.

Ghiberti's dark eyes flashed fire momentarily at her tone, then with a shrug he closed the door and strode away.

It took another fifteen minutes for Stefano to recover his composure sufficiently to leave the office, and then Pauline accompanied him over to the nursery to say goodnight to Toni before beginning his long drive back to Vernio. He kissed her when he left, and her sympathy included a share in his indignation and sense of unfairness, though she knew that Joanna was unbalanced and Niccolo innocent of any actual impropriety, just as she had assured the aggrieved husband.

Niccolo was waiting in the office when she returned.

'Who was that?' he demanded.

'Signor Sandrini,' she replied levelly. 'He's deeply upset by his wife's infatuation with you, though of course I did my best to explain the situation.'

He gasped, and this time it was his turn to redden. 'Thank you, Paolina. Actually, I think that man made a big mistake in putting his business affairs before his wife at the time of Toni's birth.'

'I'm very sorry for him—he is a nice man,' she rejoined. 'And I think you should now keep away from her, Niccolo.'

He bit his lip and frowned. 'I did what I thought best—she seemed as if she—— Yes, perhaps you're right, and I'd better avoid the poor girl.'

'Good. I think that's wise,' said Pauline quietly. 'And while we're on the subject of patients, I want to speak to you about your sister.'

'Can you not tell me over a meal in Fiesole, Paolina?'

'No, I think we might as well get it said now,' she said, fearing that the effect of his company in a more romantic atmosphere would weaken her resolve to speak her mind. 'It seems to me, Annalisa is hiding something—and I'm not convinced that she's anorexic. She enjoys certain foods, and Sister Agnello says she is eating all her chocolate bars. Tell me, Niccolo, has Annalisa had any illnesses or—or operations in recent months?'

There was a pause, and his mouth hardened into a defensive line.

'I have known my sister since her birth,' he replied coldly. 'And as a physician and surgeon, I——'

'But the very fact that she is your sister could hinder your judgement,' she ventured, thinking of the Ghiberti pride.

His brow clouded over as an idea struck him. 'Are you daring to suggest that my sister may have had an—operation that I do not know of?' He could not bring himself to say the word 'abortion'.

'No, not necessarily—though that is not impossible.' Pauline stood her ground, strengthened by her indignation on behalf of Stefano. 'Her problem may be one of a whole range of conditions.'

'Such as what?'

'That is what we hope to find out,' she replied, not willing to name any of her own suspicions without further evidence; Niccolo was, after all, well experienced in gastroenterology, and she judged that he would angrily reject any suggestion of conditions such as peptic ulcer, colitis or even malignancy as a slur on his powers of diagnosis. At the same time she knew only too well that doctors could be blind to the truth about their own close relations.

'Is that all you have to say?' he demanded.

'For the time being, yes.'

There was an uneasy pause, during which he seemed about to say something further about his sister, but he changed his mind and asked instead if she still wished to come out to dinner.

It was a challenge, she thought, and she could lose ground by putting herself in a position of obligation. She glanced at the clock on the wall.

'It's rather late now, and Toni is due for a feed,' she answered. 'Thank you all the same, Niccolo.'

'Then I will say goodnight, Pauline.' Not Paolina, she noted.

'Goodnight, Niccolo. Drive carefully!' she called after his retreating back. So that was that. Yet she did not regret her plain speaking.

The days passed quickly, and by mid-May Pauline was thoroughly at home in the surgical suite, enjoying her dual role as theatre and ward sister, and Heather had proved to be reliable and likeable once Pauline had got used to her easygoing Australian ways.

Noni settled into his new routine and began to sleep through the night, while Nina became skilled at changing his nappies and feeding him. The chubby baby took over from Dante and his *Inferno* in her affections, and she was now noticeably putting on weight. As Joanna's maternal interest revived, a relationship grew between her and the anorexic girl to their mutual advantage, and although Violetta pointed out that therapy took time, Pauline's optimism grew.

Sadly this did not apply to Annalisa, whose condition deteriorated with her moods. Sister Agnello reported that the girl would suddenly leave her drawing and disappear into the bathroom for long periods, emerging looking grey-faced and exhausted.

'Do you think she could be using purgatives?' suggested the nun. 'She could have brought a supply in with her. And she pulls such faces! It must give her a very bad pain in her tummy.'

When Niccolo told the Alberis that he intended to remove his sister from the clinic if there was no improvement by the end of another week, Pauline decided that it was time to get to the root of Annalisa's trouble as a matter of urgency. She was becoming convinced that the girl was concealing symptoms of something other than anorexia, and she decided to give her a last chance to confide in her as a friend.

That evening, after handing over to the night staff, she went to Annalisa's room, determined not to be put off, and ready to face any amount of verbal abuse if necessary. The girl was not in her room, and Pauline was about to go in search of her when Nina appeared, looking worried.

'She's in the loo at the end of the corridor, Pauline, and she must be feeling bad—she was deadly white and gritting her teeth. She's always told me not to tell anybody, but I've seen her writhing on her bed in pain. Oh, I'm so glad you're here!' confessed Nina in real distress.

Pauline at once marched along the corridor and knocked on the toilet door.

'Are you all right, Annalisa?'

A weak voice answered with a rude Italian expression which meant 'go away', followed by a low, agonised groan.

'Go and get Dr Alberi, and tell him to bring the master key,' Pauline ordered Nina, suddenly aware that there was no time to lose.

'For God's sake be sensible and turn the lock, Annalisa—can't you understand that I'm your friend?' she pleaded.

There was another groan, and a muttered '*Non posso*——' ending in silence. Pauline was by now frightened, and when Riccardo and Jenny came running along the corridor she was trembling with dread at what they would find.

'Quick, unlock this door!' she told Riccardo. 'Annalisa's very ill!'

He opened the toilet with the key, and Pauline rushed in.

There was an unpleasant and characteristic odour, and Annalisa lay sprawled on the floor. Pauline stared at the evidence that confirmed her half-formed suspicions—the blood and mucus typical of advanced bowel inflammation.

Riccardo quickly knelt beside the feebly moaning girl, feeling for her pulse and raising her head up from the floor.

'What do you know about this?' he asked Pauline in horrified tones.

'I think she has ulcerative colitis,' said Pauline, her voice shaking. 'She needs urgent treatment—surgery, probably.'

He nodded. 'I'll get on to Santa Maria Nuova—and Niccolo.'

Annalisa stirred and opened her eyes, which were full of fear. 'No, no, don't tell my brother,' she whispered in Italian. 'He'd make me have a horrible colostomy, and I'd rather die.'

As Riccardo lifted the girl in his arms Pauline at last began to realise something of the agony that Niccolo's sister had suffered in her desperate attempt to conceal her symptoms.

And her own failure to gain Annalisa's trust and allay her fears. Had she left it too late?

CHAPTER EIGHT

PAULINE thought she would never forget the look on Niccolo's face when he came to Annalisa's bedside in the surgical suite. Fear and self-accusation in equal measure had drained his features of colour and expression, and the resemblance between the brother and sister now seemed more marked. The girl's transparent pallor, outlined by her dark hair, matched the pillows on which she lay with eyes closed, her insubstantial frame like a child's beneath the featherweight duvet. Riccardo had commenced an intravenous infusion of glucose and saline solution into her left arm, which lay splinted upon the turned back sheet.

For the twentieth time that evening Pauline asked herself why she had not been more alert to the signs of an acute organic condition, and Annalisa's rapid deterioration during the past week. The girl had managed to deceive them all, diverting attention away from the telltale signs of inflammatory bowel disease by playing the part of a neurotic; she had used her considerable acting ability to manipulate all her carers—including her brother.

Especially her brother, reflected Pauline, because of his profession; it had been his reaction that Annalisa had most feared.

Pauline had returned to the surgical suite to act as special nurse to Annalisa until a specialist arrived to examine her and decide what treatment was necessary; she was in the act of recording temperature, pulse

and blood pressure when Niccolo quietly came in with
Riccardo. It was five to ten, and he had driven up
from Florence as soon as he had received Riccardo's
summons.

'The consultant surgeon is coming to see her, and
will probably want her transferred to Santa Maria
Nuova,' whispered Riccardo to Pauline as Niccolo
gazed down at his sister. 'I'd better go and keep an
eye open for him,' he added as he left them.

'Annalisa.' Niccolo uttered her name with an effort,
glancing at Pauline as he spoke, as if seeking
reassurance.

'Annalisa, why didn't you tell me? Why—why could
you not trust your own brother?' The raw pain in the
words touched Pauline's heart, but she kept silent;
Annalisa opened her eyes and slowly focused them
upon Niccolo.

'I don't want to be mutilated,' she whispered, turning
her face away from him.

'But *cara mia*, this can be cured—you can recover
and live a normal life——' he began, taking hold of
her right hand.

She moved her head and turned her huge eyes upon
him in weary defiance.

'Don't speak of it to me, Niccolo,' she told him in
Italian. 'Pauline knows I'd rather die than have a hole
in my body where it shouldn't be.'

She closed her eyes as if the effort of speaking had
taken what strength she had left. Pauline forced a
smile, and felt it her duty to speak on the patient's
behalf.

'Don't say any more now, please, Niccolo. We
mustn't upset her.'

She was surprised at the degree of quiet authority

in her tone, and Niccolo must have heard it too because he deferred to her as if he were any other worried relative with no medical knowledge at all. He drew up a chair and sat down on the other side of the bed.

Pauline passed him the charts on which basic recordings had been commenced, and a few minutes passed in silence, ended by the arrival of the consultant gastroenterologist from Florence, accompanied by Riccardo. Niccolo was politely but firmly dismissed while a careful examination was made and a case-history taken in the form of a series of sensitively phrased questions.

Annalisa answered obediently enough, though very slowly. All the fight seemed to have gone out of her, as if she had given up the struggle against an enemy whose insidious advance she was powerless to stop. She admitted that the symptoms had started over a year ago with tiredness, weight-loss and recurrent bouts of diarrhoea with pain, and that she had told no one when she had started passing blood. She had taken proprietary medicines with no effect—and her fear of surgical intervention amounted to an obsession.

Pauline reproached herself all over again as she listened. If only she had known! She could have quoted to Annalisa, in confidence, the names of certain well-known people, some in the world of entertainment and even sport, who had needed to have a colostomy or ileostomy—an artificial bowel opening, either temporary or permanent—and had continued to lead their lives as usual, undeterred by what Annalisa considered a mutilation.

So much fear is based on ignorance and prejudice, thought Pauline sadly, and resolved that from then on she would do everything she could to educate Annalisa Ghiberti towards a more positive outlook.

If it was not too late. . .

The surgeon ended his palpation of Annalisa's tummy, discovering acute tenderness over the affected area, and when a rectal examination was very gently carried out there was further evidence of internal bleeding. He looked grave, and spoke with kind but uncompromising directness.

'I shall need to take you into hospital in Florence for tests that cannot be done here, *signorina*,' he told the girl. 'Depending on the results, I shall make a decision whether or not to operate, all right?'

Annalisa merely shook her head and closed her eyes.

A consultation took place in the office between the surgeon, Riccardo and Niccolo. A painkilling sedative injection was ordered, which Pauline gave, and arrangements were made to have the patient transferred by ambulance on the following morning to Santa Maria Nuova.

It was past eleven when Pauline left the suite and went to collect Toni from his nursery to take him to her room for the night as usual.

However, she found that his mother was reluctant to let him go. He had recently been fed, and was sleeping peacefully in his cot beside Joanna's bed. She begged Pauline to let him stay, and her special nurse, Guilia, supported her plea.

'I feel braver when my baby's near me, Sister, and I'm learning all over again to be a mother to him,' said Joanna, looking rather bewilderedly at the nurse she had once known as a close friend. 'I change him and give him the bottle myself now, don't I, Guilia?'

'Yes—she's getting better every day, Infermiera Stephens,' agreed the auxiliary nurse entrusted with round-the-clock observation of the *signora*, and

Pauline had to make a decision. Perhaps the time had now come to give Toni back into his mother's care, under the supervision of the devoted and trustworthy Guilia, who would remain in the room throughout the night.

'All right, Joanna, dear, if you're sure that's what you want,' she said gently, thankful for these signs of a return to normality. 'And by the way, how is your husband these days? Has he been to see you lately?'

'Oh, yes, my Stefano is most kind, and supported me very well when I was ill,' replied the mother. 'And if you don't mind me reminding you, Sister, my name is Giovanna—Signora Giovanna Sandrini, to distinguish me from my mother-in-law, also Signora Sandrini, you see.'

'*Si, Giovanna*,' smiled Pauline, wondering if her friend was gradually coming to terms with her new nationality and status as part of the long road back to mental health. Thank heaven for that much, anyway!

More tired than she had realised, she continued on her way to the staff quarters, cutting across the shrubbery at the back of the main block.

'Paolina!'

She stopped at once, her heart missing a beat.

'Niccolo—*buona sera*!' she exclaimed as he emerged from the shadows where he had been waiting for her. 'Are you staying here tonight?'

'Yes, Riccardo has offered me a room, and I'll accompany Annalisa in the ambulance tomorrow,' he replied quickly. 'But if it's not too late, Paolina, I must speak with you—though I hardly know how to find words to tell you my thoughts tonight.'

His manner was uncharacteristically agitated, and in the half-dark of the summer night his eyes were two

pools reflecting his inner turmoil. For the second time
that evening Pauline felt that she must take control and
steer the conversation into calm and sensible channels.

'Of course—I'm here to listen, Niccolo,' she said
with deliberate ease and informality, though she felt
anything but easy beneath the surface. 'Let's take a
stroll through the garden, shall we? Though we'd better
not talk too loudly at this hour!'

Whether she took his hand or he took hers she was
never quite sure, but they found themselves walking
hand in hand through the shrubbery and along
the mosaic paving around the now covered
swimming-pool.

'We might as well sit down.' She smiled as they came
to a wooden bench set back from the pool; the sun-beds
and loungers had all been put away. Paolina, I——'
He bit back what he had been about to say, and his
fingers gripped hers almost painfully. She firmly took
his right hand between her own.

'Niccolo, we're *all* reproaching ourselves about
Annalisa, if that's what troubling you,' she said very
quietly.

'But of *course* it's troubling me!' he retorted with
emotion, turning to face her as if she had accused him.
'I feel no longer a doctor. I cannot see what is in front
of my eyes. I—I have been so blind! When you tried
to tell me I was so arrogant, a complete fool—and
I've been no good to poor Signora Sandrini, either.
Oh, Paolina, tell me what I shall do if my sister dies—
because that is a possibility now—and I will have let
her die, because I refused to see what was happening
to her. *O mio Dio!*'

'*Rubbish*, Niccolo—*sciocchezze*! All right, so you
were mistaken—which proves that you are just another

fallible human being like the rest of us,' she said emphatically. 'We *all* make mistakes, and the only thing we can do is to learn from them, right? Listen, Niccolo, you must get a hold on yourself. All this self-reproach and accusation will be no good to your sister. I feel that I failed with her too, but not entirely—at least we got her into the right place, didn't we? Even though she fooled us all—Riccardo and Violetta and Sister Agnello—and me! None of us got through to her and understood the fear she was battling with. But now that she's to have all these tests and expert assessment——'

He seized her hands and looked deep into her eyes under the midnight sky.

'But is there still time to save her? The bowel could perforate, and she could haemorrhage to death——'

Pauline took a deep breath and summoned up all the courage and common sense she possessed for the sake of this man.

'We must pray that there *is* still time, Niccolo, and help Annalisa by keeping our heads. You must be brave,' she commanded.

'And you must help me, Paolina—you must help me, I implore you!' He spoke wildly, gripping her shoulder.

It was heartrending to see the Ghiberti pride brought so low, and the temptation to put her arms around him and hold him close was almost overpowering, but Pauline reined in her emotions with a superhuman effort; now was not the right time.

'Steady, Niccolo—I'll help you all I can, but you must stop blaming yourself. You are not the first doctor to fail to diagnose a member of your own family—I've seen it happen before. Annalisa is very special to you, I know,' she said, lowering her eyes to hide the yearning tenderness in them.

'But I have not understood her thoughts, Paolina. I have not looked and listened as a doctor should,' he said despairingly.

'Does anybody ever fully understand another human being, Niccolo?' she asked. 'Look at poor Stefano Sandrini, who loves his wife but has been completely baffled by her state of mind.'

'And a lot of help *I* was there,' he rejoined bitterly.

'Actually, Dr Luongo thinks you *were* good for her during that acute phase when she first came here—and you couldn't have responded in any other way,' said Pauline comfortingly, forgetting her own hurt resentment at the time, and Stefano's jealousy.

He put an arm around her shoulders, and for a while they sat there on the bench under the midnight sky. Pauline secretly rejoiced in his closeness, his obvious need for her reassurance at this time of crisis; she could only hope and pray that she would not fail him.

'It's time we turned in now, Niccolo,' she said at last, reluctant though she was to end this precious moment. 'Tomorrow will be a long day.'

'Yes, I must let you go. *Di nuovo, molte grazie, Paolina, cara mia.*'

And he gave her the grateful kiss of a friend, heartfelt but not demanding.

After Annalisa's transfer to the university hospital the Alberis and Pauline anxiously awaited the results of a whole battery of tests and investigations. They saw nothing of Niccolo, although he telephoned Riccardo daily with news of his sister.

It was not encouraging. Blood tests showed con-

tinued severe anaemia and electrolyte imbalance,
though liver function was normal. A straight abdominal
X-ray showed distension of the toxic colon, and an
exploration under a general anaesthetic confirmed the
advanced ulceration. Surgery was advised—removal of
the diseased part of the colon, or large intestine—with
a colostomy for three to six months, depending on
progress.

Nina burst into tears when Pauline told her the news,
for she was yet another person racked with self-blame
over the whole sorry affair.

'If only I had not promised not to tell Dr Alberi or
anybody about the pain I knew she was suffering, I
could have alerted you all at least two weeks ago!' she
sobbed.

'It's difficult when you've given your word to a
friend, Nina,' sighed Pauline, whose thoughts were
hourly with the brother and sister—though she had to
continue her work as usual, with all its physical and
emotional demands.

She missed her contact with Toni as his mother took
over his care, but was thankful for a good night's rest
again—especially as Kitty O'Hare left the clinic at the
end of May, leaving Pauline and Heather as the only
theatre nurses, assisted by an auxiliary and the wizard
male orderly who kept all the fixtures and appliances
in good working order, and always changed the gas
cylinders just before they became empty.

On a beautiful day at the beginning of June Riccardo
received a message from the consultant surgeon, asking
if he would be willing to have Signorina Ghiberti back
at the Clinico Silverio for a course of intensive medication and conservative treatment. He had yielded to
her plea for a week's reprieve from surgery, and had

agreed to her return to the clinic, provided that Dr Alberi consented.

And of course he *did*, though Pauline hardly knew whether to be pleased or sorry; the responsibility would be enormous. Her determination rose to the challenge, and on the following Monday morning the ambulance arrived with Annalisa, whose physical condition appeared unchanged though mentally she was a different girl.

She was now co-operative and willing to undergo the rigorous routine of blood transfusions and other intravenous fluids, and the cortisone treatment given in the form of a daily enema—a foaming preparation which Pauline administered and Annalisa uncomplainingly endured. Intravenous vitamin supplements and a range of antibiotics were used to build up the patient and prevent infections, while her diet was a high-calorie and low-residue programme, mainly in the form of milky liquids. Strict fluid balance was maintained, and the surgeon called daily to pore over the many charts recording her progress.

It was the hardest week of Pauline's life as a nurse. She had to be ruthless with visitors, including Niccolo, to maintain an atmosphere of quiet calm at all times. Tapes of the girl's favourite music were played at low volume, and Sister Agnello came to read stories and poems in her cool, soothing nun's voice. The priest also visited daily, and Annalisa made her confession and received Holy Communion. Everything that could possibly have been done to arrest the disease and save an operation was done, and by the end of each day Pauline felt drained of all her vitality, so great were the emotional demands made on her.

'Are you sure it's not too much for you, love?' asked

Jenny anxiously. 'Can't Heather take a turn?'

'No, Heather's great at running the suite, and the patients like her—only she's too boisterous to spend hours with Annalisa every day,' replied Pauline firmly. 'Don't worry, Jenny, I'm fine—and you know I'd do anything—absolutely *anything* for Niccolo, and that includes his sister.'

'I know, and that's what worries me,' murmured Jenny, who, like Riccardo, did not have high expectations of the conservative treatment, and feared the effect of strain and overwork on Pauline.

The Tuesday, Wednesday, Thursday and Friday of that critical week passed in monotonous succession. Pauline saw Niccolo watching for signs of improvement, and her heart twisted as his hopes faded when there was no reversal of the disease. The consultant's face was unsmiling as he ordered yet another blood transfusion on the Friday night, and by morning Annalisa's pulse was rapid and her blood pressure dangerously low.

A hasty consultation took place between the surgeon and Riccardo, and Pauline heard the words 'failure to respond'—'imminent perforation and peritonitis'—'urgent need for intervention' exchanged in muttered Italian phrases. Niccolo was called in to hear the news he had already guessed. He took it stoically, agreeing that if an operation had to be done, then the sooner the better.

But where? To subject the patient to another ambulance journey in her present condition was thought to be too risky, though such a serious operation as was proposed had never been previously performed at the Clinico Silverio. Pauline hardly dared to look at Niccolo as the pros and cons were swiftly weighed up, a decision made, and preparations set in motion for an emergency removal of half the colon in the clinic's little theatre at midday on that same Saturday, when the consultant surgeon had no ward-round, out-patients' clinic or operation list at Santa Maria Nuova.

Riccardo was to give the anaesthetic, but no second surgeon was available to assist, so Niccolo was asked if he would be willing to scrub up with the consultant. He at once agreed, and although the surgeon would have preferred somebody other than a close relative of the patient, there was no time for debating the matter. Pauline was scheduled to act as theatre sister, with a staff nurse as 'runner' and the male orderly as a back-up assistant.

A further six half-litres of blood were crossmatched and sent up to the clinic on the supplies van, along with some special equipment which included colostomy drainage bags and other items for post-operative care. During the past five days Pauline had only briefly touched on this subject, as Annalisa had been so deter-mined to avoid the operation; now there was almost no time left other than the couple of hours during which she must be prepared for surgery, and Pauline feared that she might refuse to sign her consent. In fact there was no problem over this.

'They tell me it need only be temporary, Pauline. I don't know if they are telling me the truth or not—but I might as well go through with it now,' said the girl with a fatalistic air as she scrawled her name on the form held in front of her.

Pauline helped her to put on the cotton gown and tuck her hair into a turban-style cap, then a catheter had to be passed into her bladder.

'Now for an injection to send you floating away on

a fluffy little cloud, dear,' said Pauline, amazed at her own calmness at this moment, and privately sending up a fervent prayer for them all.

On the stroke of midday the trolley was wheeled into the theatre where the three gowned, gloved and masked figures stood waiting. Riccardo and the orderly transferred the unconscious patient on to the operating table, and Pauline quickly painted the skin of the abdomen with a pink antiseptic dye. Green operating towels were draped in position, leaving a square aperture over where the incision was to be made.

'*Tutto pronto*?' asked the surgeon, glancing at Niccolo, who nodded, then at Pauline, who was ready with her instruments.

'*Va bene, cominciamo*,' he murmured, and the life-saving operation began.

Little was said as they worked in close co-operation for the next hour. Riccardo, as anaesthetist, was in charge of the blood transfusion and a simultaneous intravenous line for other fluids and medication.

After the greater part of the colon had been removed, the lower cut end was sealed and closed, while the upper end was brought out through a small incision on the left side of the abdomen. Pauline looked at this colostomy which Annalisa had so much dreaded, and handed the surgeon a plastic drainage tube to insert into it before a dressing was applied. The long incision was closed in layers, with a row of stitches on the surface.

'*E' finito*,' said the surgeon, stepping back and spreading out his hands. '*Molte grazie, signori e signore*.'

Pauline's eyes met Niccolo's above their surgical

mask, and their unspoken thoughts were identical. The operation might be finished, but for Annalisa life with a colostomy was about to begin.

And neither of them was sure that she would be able to cope.

Back in her room, surrounded by drip-stands, bladder and wound-drainage-tubes, Annalisa stirred in the haze of painkilling medication given before she left the theatre.

'*Dov'è sono?*' she whispered, unable to remember anything that had happened that day, though both Niccolo and Pauline were there to assure her that she had come safely through her operation, and that everything was fine.

'Don't try to talk, dear,' said Pauline in Italian, offering a sip of iced water to moisten the girl's lips. 'Just close your eyes and sleep again now.'

But before she drifted away back to sleep, Annalisa Ghiberti smiled at her brother and Pauline—a smile that lit up her big eyes and softened the thin features that had so long been tensely defiant.

'You are so good to me,' she murmured as her eyes closed. Pauline found that her own eyes were suddenly misty, and she felt that she should leave the brother and sister alone for a short while. Murmuring something about having to check the theatre, she quietly left the room, and, not wishing to run into Heather or anybody else just then, she slipped along to the empty theatre and closed the door behind her.

Her pent-up emotion had been suppressed for so long, and now, in this place where she had made her vital contribution to the saving of Niccolo's sister's life, her self-control faltered, and she gave way to a moment of relief and deep thankfulness. She leaned her elbows upon the operating table and let her head fall between her hands.

She did not hear the door silently open, or the muffled sound of rubber soles on the tiled floor. She only felt the two strong arms that slid round her waist as she drooped over the table, and heard the whispered words against the back of her neck.

'*Oh, Paolina, cara mia. . .*'

Her body straightened up like a flower reviving in rain; she turned round within the circle of his arms to see his face, and for a timeless moment they clung together.

'I shall never be able to thank you enough——' he began, but words were lost as their lips met. His hands moved up to her shoulders and came to rest on each side of her head, cupping her face as he kissed her, drinking deeply of her sweetness. All her tension and tiredness melted in the surge of mutual emotion that mingled the tears on their cheeks. . .

They sprang apart when they heard Heather Hulland's knock on the door.

'Hell, I'm sorry, Pauline, but is she to have the next half-litre of packed cells straight away, or shall I put up Hartmann's solution next?' asked the Australian girl apologetically.

Pauline hurried back to Annalisa's room without having said a word to Niccolo; she reflected once again that this was not the right time for indulging in an impassioned reaction, not when her skill and undivided attention was required by Niccolo's sister.

Annalisa's recovery from major abdominal surgery was slow, but the change in her mental attitude was a significant factor in her progress. Intensive nursing care was still needed, and Pauline took charge of the colostomy for the first week, not requiring the girl to do anything other than watch as Pauline changed the dressings and placed the squares of pliable, toffee-coloured karaya over the surrounding skin.

'Marvellous stuff, this—comes from an Indian tree,' she said in matter-of-fact tones. 'It sticks firmly to your tummy, but peels off easily—see? And it's actually good for your skin, keeps it from getting sore.'

The day came when intravenous drips and drainage-tubes could all be removed and the colostomy began to function, which meant that Annalisa could start eating small amounts of easily digested food. To eat without fear of pain was a welcome experience, and her appetite improved rapidly.

Holding on to Pauline's arm, she took slow, uncertain steps, gaining confidence as she tottered along until she could leave her room and sit outside in the June sunshine. Nina was constantly at her side, and Maria and Elena came to visit. Maria felt that she had been vindicated for writing to Niccolo, and proudly gave herself credit for the happy outcome; Pauline smiled indulgently, remembering that it had been Maria who had got her into the Palazzo Alessandra.

One day, when Niccolo found his sister's room vacant, he went to the office of the surgical suite where Pauline sat typing data into the computer.

'So where have you taken her this afternoon?' he asked with a smile.

Pauline stood up and beckoned him to follow her out through the shrubbery to where a delightful picture could be seen beside the pool.

Annalisa and Nina reclined on sun-loungers while Giovanna Sandrini shared a wooden bench with Jenny, now blooming in her twenty-eighth week of pregnancy. All four of them were devoting themselves to the one male member of the group, a bonny ten-week-old baby wearing only a plastic-backed nappy and a little striped cotton vest.

'It's a meeting of the Antonio Sandrini fan-club, and you may find that the members aren't able to detach themselves from him,' warned Pauline.

Ghiberti gazed at the group in wonder. 'Whoever would have thought to see this, even a month ago?' he marvelled in a low tone.

'My sister is smiling at the baby, forgetting all about her problems—and just look at Joanna—I mean Giovanna—showing off her baby with pride! And Nina too—she has put on much weight, though she is looking a little wistful, yes?'

'She knows that she'll have to part with Toni soon,' explained Pauline. 'He and his mother will probably be discharged at the weekend. Giovanna is still on anti-depressants, and will need to be closely followed up, but she's gradually getting back to normal. Stefano is over the moon, and—— Oh, look, he's come to visit them—*buongiorno*, Signor Sandrini!'

The two men shook hands rather awkwardly, and exchanged conventional greetings. Stefano could hardly wait to see his wife and son, while Annalisa gave her brother an affectionate kiss. Pauline felt a little out of this happy scene of reunion, but Giovanna suddenly detached herself from Stefano's embrace, gave Toni to Nina to hold, and came to Pauline's side.

'I do hope that we can be friends again—I'm so sorry if I've treated you badly, Pauline,' she said earnestly. 'I have been on a dark journey in my head, and couldn't find my way. I thought you had deserted me, and I was so frightened—it was terrible! But now it's like the sun coming out, and I can see things clearly again—I'm coming back to the real world!'

Pauline was moved at this graphic description of postnatal depression.

'Oh, Jo, please, don't say any more,' she begged. 'I'm just so happy to have you back again as my friend!' And they exchanged a kiss and a hug.

Stefano came over and put an arm around each of them, all smiles.

'We have come through it together, yes? And I tell you, I shall never leave my Giovanna for any long business trips again. She and my son are much too precious. You see, I too have learned some lessons, yes?'

'It looks as if happy endings are in sight, Paolina, but it will take time,' whispered Niccolo. 'Annalisa and Nina still have to come to terms with their lives, and Giovanna will need to be very carefully watched when she becomes pregnant again.'

Pauline nodded. 'But let's enjoy this lovely afternoon, Niccolo, and look at the progress they've made, all three of them.'

'*Si*, Paolina, but I shall not be able to look at them for much longer. It has been eight weeks since I returned to Florence, and with Annalisa now doing well, I have to return to finish my exchange year at Beltonshaw.'

A cloud drifted across the sun, and Pauline gave an involuntary gasp of dismay.

'Oh, er—yes, I see. When must you go?' she asked, trying not to sound as dejected as she felt at the prospect of Florence without Niccolo.

'I have promised to be back in the last week of this

month, so I have booked a flight from Pisa on the twenty-first,' he told her.

'So soon! What a lot has happened in these few short weeks,' reflected Pauline, who might have been here half her working life, so at home did she feel.

'Perhaps a little too much has happened,' murmured Niccolo with a sigh, making her wonder what he meant. He squeezed her arm gently as he went on.

'I feel much happier about leaving Annalisa, knowing that you and the Alberis will be caring for her. I tell you, Paolina, I shall return to Beltonshaw in a better heart than when I left it.'

That may be so, thought Pauline bleakly, but it means *addio*—goodbye again until next year.

Which was a very long time.

CHAPTER NINE

THE sunny June days sped by all too quickly, and while Annalisa daily gained strength and new confidence in herself Pauline had to hide her sadness as the day of Niccolo's departure approached. He managed to visit his sister on most days, though sometimes only very briefly, and always exchanged a few words with Pauline on these occasions. But there was none of that closeness, that tender intimacy which had so melted her heart and led to dreams of a future spent together in Florence—for Pauline had let herself imagine what life might be like as a wife, as a *signora*.

As Signora Paolina Ghiberti. . .

But it seemed that Niccolo had decided to put a brake on their relationship, which had accelerated during the anxious days before and after Annalisa's operation. What had he said that afternoon beside the pool? 'Perhaps a little too much has happened.' She had wondered then what he meant, but now the meaning appeared to be all too clear. With his sister well on the road to recovery, he was able to stop worrying about her and blaming himself on her account; he was no longer dependent upon Pauline's support.

And, of course, he had to return to his exchange registrarship at Beltonshaw and make up the ten weeks he had lost, which would bring him to the end of the following April—another good reason for not committing himself to a serious relationship at this point in his life. Especially with a girl of different nationality—a girl he had met less than three months ago, and who was presumptuously dreaming of herself as Signora Ghiberti!

Pauline raised her chin and pushed her shoulders back in a gesture of resolution. All right, so Niccolo thought he had gone too far with her, and now wanted time to reconsider, but there was no doubt that the Alberis needed her—especially with Nurse O'Hara gone and Jenny getting noticeably bigger and feeling the heat. Riccardo was relying on Pauline more than Jenny to take charge of the nursing care at the clinic during his brief absences. He had also asked if she would extend her contract for a further six months, and she was still considering this.

Suddenly it was the day before Niccolo's flight from Pisa. Pauline was certain that he would come to say goodbye and exchange a few words with her in private. Would he kiss her? Oh, surely he would hold her close just for a moment and whisper '*Paolina, cara mia*'—wouldn't he?

There were three operations scheduled for that morning, and the surgeon from Fiesole was delayed, so the list did not start until past eleven and went on until nearly two. When Pauline left the theatre she first had to check on the condition of the three post-operative patients, and then went over to the staff quarters to take a shower. She put on a clean white cotton dress and made her way to Annalisa's room with a pounding heart. Niccolo would probably be already there. . .

'Oh, Pauline, where have you been? You missed Niccolo!' cried Annalisa. 'He had to leave because he has much to do and is on duty this evening. He ask me to say goodbye and give you this letter.'

She stared at Pauline's stricken face as she held out the envelope.

'Are you well, Pauline?' she asked as the letter was put into the pocket of the white dress. Pauline had momentarily closed her eyes, but quickly recovered her composure.

'Thank you, Annalisa, it's all right. I know I'm a little late after the operation list,' she said lightly, forcing a smile. 'You needed to see your brother alone on his last visit. Now, how are you feeling? I believe that Dr Alberi is talking about discharging you to your flat next week?'

'Yes, as long as I can cope with the—the colostomy on my own,' answered the girl, clearly seeking reassurance.

'Well, you can certainly manage *that*, you've been marvellous,' smiled Pauline, acting as if her heart was not breaking inside her. All she longed for was the privacy of her room, where she could collapse on the bed and try to recover from this body-blow.

He had not waited for her. He had not even said goodbye. And surely he could not be on duty for Pronto Soccorso on the very eve of his departure!

'Are you sure you are all right, Pauline?' Annalisa asked again, looking at her closely. Her brother had seemed agitated when he visited, and now Pauline also seemed unsettled. 'You have been so good to us, Pauline, and I wish that—I mean, I've hoped that perhaps you and——'

'Oh, don't say it, Annalisa!' Pauline cut in. 'It just doesn't matter now. I'm sure that you and I will always be friends, whatever happens.'

'Yes, we will,' said the girl thoughtfully. 'And I'd

like to ask you a question if you don't mind, Pauline. Tell me, just suppose that I *do* have to live with this colostomy for the rest of my life—does that mean I could never have a baby?'

There was a desperate plea in the question, and Pauline turned round slowly to look straight into the eyes of Niccolo's sister.

'Oh, my dear, is *that* what's been worrying you all this time?' she said, instinctively putting her patient's need before her own troubled mind. She sat down on the side of the bed.

'Why did you never ask before, Annalisa? A woman with a permanent colostomy can certainly get married, and some have had children. It's not very common, but I know a midwife who attended one. The baby was born by Caesarean section, and everything was fine. Listen, Annalisa, let me explain. . .'

And, taking hold of the girl's hand, she answered all the worrying questions as completely as she could.

'And in any case, you'll almost certainly be able to have this colostomy closed long before the problem arises,' she concluded. 'Especially if you go on making such good progress!'

'Pauline, you are an *angel*!'

The two girls exchanged a sisterly kiss just as Nina arrived, giving Pauline her chance at last to go and read Niccolo's letter.

'Ask Nina about her plans to return to university in the autumn!' she said, and hurried away to her room where with shaking hands she tore open the envelope. The words on the single sheet swam before her eyes and did not at first make sense; sentences stood out here and there, and she stared at them, only half comprehending their meaning.

'. . .what you have done for Annalisa and myself. . . yet I have to return to Manchester until next spring. . .my commitments, and uncertainty about the future. . .perhaps best that we should part at this time. . .heartfelt wishes for your future happiness. . .ever your grateful friend, Niccolo Ghiberti.'

'Oh, no. No. Not like this, Niccolo,' she whispered aloud as the sentences added up to the unmistakable message of farewell. It was true, then. He did not want to see her again.

She sat on the bed and stared into space until a gentle tap on the door roused her from the mental blankness that had overtaken her.

'Pauline, dear, may I come in?'

It was Jenny, looking concerned as she quietly entered the room.

'I saw you on your way up here, love, and thought you looked a bit down,' she said softly. 'Want to tell Auntie Jenny about it?'

Pauline silently handed the letter to her friend, who sat down beside her and read it. For a full minute neither of them spoke, and then Jenny burst out in indignation.

'My God! It's too bad of him, Pauline—those damned Ghibertis! They'll never change. When I think of what that man owes to you—oh, you're better off without him!' she almost shouted, her face flushed with anger.

'No, Jenny, he has his reasons, and no man is obliged to marry a woman just because she loves him,' said Pauline sadly. 'He's never really encouraged me to——' And she gave way to the tears that had been held back for so long. Jenny put her arms around her friend's heaving shoulders and comforted her as well as she could.

'I *must* see him before he goes, Jenny,' muttered Pauline. 'I want to hear his reasons from his own lips—and I have a right to say goodbye, after all that's happened. I have to see him, just once before he gets on the plane.'

'I don't think that would be wise, love,' cautioned her friend. 'You'll only be more upset, and end up wishing you'd kept away.'

'No, he owes me this much, Jen,' resolved Pauline, drying her eyes. 'Is it all right if I take the rest of the day off? Heather's got the surgical suite organised, and the post-ops are fine. I can get a bus down into the city and walk up from the Duomo to the hospital. Even if he's on duty, I'll wait in Pronto Soccorso until he's free.'

Jenny saw that it was no use arguing. 'All right, love, but I've got two things to say. A—you're making a mistake, and B—as you're determined to make it, I'll come with you. No, don't try to put me off—we can go in Riccardo's car. I'm not letting you go out alone in this state. I won't intrude on your privacy, but I'll lurk in the background, OK?'

After a quick word with a disapproving Riccardo, the girls set off down the zig-zag road, and Jenny found a place to park the car near to the Piazza Santa Maria Nuova, from where they walked to the entrance of Pronto Soccorso.

'I'll rest here while you beard the dragon in his den,' panted Jenny, sitting down breathlessly just outside. 'I'll give you half an hour to find him and hear him out, and remember I'm waiting here for you, whatever happens, right? Go on, then—and good luck!'

But Jenny had only to wait five minutes before Pauline returned, white-faced and with a firmly set mouth.

'What happened? Did you see him?' queried Jenny, almost afraid to ask.

'No, Jen, he's gone. Packed and left. Finished his job here and gone to his home, wherever that is,' replied Pauline in a flat and unemotional tone.

'Well, of all the—— So much for him saying he was on duty this evening,' seethed Jenny, restrained by Pauline's face from giving full vent to her thoughts. 'Look, love, let's go for a wander around the shops now we're here, and find a nice *trattoria*. I don't know about you, but I could down a cup of good English tea. Come on!'

Pauline took her arm and they walked down to the fashion centre of Florence, where Jenny pointed out the elegant creations on display in shop windows.

'Violetta Luongo got a simply gorgeous hat here in the Via de' Tornabuoni last week—I wouldn't mind trying one on, would you?' she suggested in an effort to divert her friend.

'*Mi scusi, Signorina Stephens—come sta*?' a male voice enquired.

Pauline turned round sharply at hearing herself addressed, and saw a dark-eyed, handsome young man smiling at her in delight. His right leg was encased in a plaster, and he walked with crutches.

'*Enrico*! *Buongiorno*! *Sto bene, grazie. E come stai*?' she replied, using the more familiar form of greeting. They stood on the pavement conversing in Italian for his benefit, and he plucked up the courage to ask a favour of her.

'I want so much to write to the Signor and Signora

Partridge, and tell them how sorry I am for causing the accident to the Signora,' he confided. 'Please, *signorina*, will you help me to write a letter in English to beg for their forgiveness?'

Pauline had to smile at his earnestness. 'Yes, of course I'll help you, Enrico. Write a letter in your own words and send it to me at the Clinico Silverio near Fiesole. I will translate it into English and send it to them care of their travel company. No problem!'

'*Molte grazie, cara signorina, molte——*' began Enrico, but stopped and stared in alarm at Jenny, who was clutching at her tummy with one hand and at Pauline with the other. Her face was contorted in agony.

'I—I'm sorry, Pauline, but—such a *pain*—help me!' she implored.

The next few minutes were like a bad dream. Jenny sank down on the pavement with a moan and knelt awkwardly, her head and shoulders drooping as she gasped with pain and fear. Horrified, Pauline knelt down beside her in the street.

'When did the pain start, Jen?' she asked, willing herself to stay calm.

'Just now. It simply came on—a really awful pain in my back and all down my side. Oh, get Riccardo, *please*!' Her voice rose hysterically.

'Don't panic, love, I'll take care of you and get Riccardo just as soon as——' began Pauline, but was interrupted by Enrico, who leaned over her with unexpected authority and declared that her friend needed an ambulance to take her to hospital.

'*Telefono subito per un' ambulanza, dal negozio,*' he said, explaining that he would telephone from the department store outside which they had been talking.

He hobbled through the impressive doors, deftly manipulating his crutches.

A crowd had gathered around the two young women, and Pauline asked for assistance to get her friend into the fashionable store, where they could await the ambulance. To her relief a burly man stepped forward, and together they lifted Jenny up to a standing position and walked her slowly through the doors; a flustered store manageress brought her a chair.

'How's the pain now, Jenny?' asked Pauline, praying that the baby was not on its way. With ten weeks still to go, it was much too early for a safe birth, especially here in the Via de' Tornabuoni.

'It's a little easier, but I feel so strange—kind of light-headed,' groaned Jenny, leaning forward on the chair and holding her tummy as if to protect her baby. Pauline took her pulse, and Enrico hovered near them, assuring them that an ambulance was on its way with a doctor who had been warned of the *signora's* condition.

'Have you felt the baby moving lately?' Pauline asked her friend.

'I think so. Oh, Pauline, do you think it'll be all right?'

'Yes, love, try not to worry, just keep still and—'

'*L'ambulanza è arrivata*!' announced the manageress, and to Pauline's enormous relief she saw the olive-green van drawing up outside. She dashed out to meet the hooded figure who jumped down from the passenger seat while his driver began removing a stretcher from the back of the van.

'*Buongiorno, Fratello*!' she greeted him, thankful beyond words for the renowned Brotherhood, always ready to answer a distress call from their station in the Piazza del Duomo.

'*Buongiorno. Sono un dottore. Dov'è la signora in parto prematuro?*' he demanded.

Pauline stopped short at the sound of that voice, and her brain whirled. She stared up at the tall man who had come to answer Enrico's summons.

'Niccolo!'

'Paolina!' he exclaimed.

'Oh, Niccolo, it's Jenny Alberi—she's in terrible pain, and the baby's not due for another ten weeks!'

'Jenny? *O mio Dio—andiamo!*' He followed her swiftly into the store, where a wide-eyed Jenny looked up in astonishment.

'Dr Ghiberti! So you *were* on an evening shift—with the Brotherhood of Mercy!' she groaned.

He smiled at her and placed a firm hand on her tummy. 'Any loss of blood, *signora*? Or water?'

'There's no blood,' whispered Pauline, 'though there is some wetness. I'm not sure if her membranes have broken. It's the severity of the pain that literally brought her to her knees.'

'We had better get her into the van and away to Santa Maria Nuova for a complete examination, yes?'

Beckoning to the driver who had come in carrying the stretcher, he and Pauline helped Jenny to lie down on it. The two men then carried her out to the van.

'You come too, Paolina, yes?' he said. 'You can call Dr Alberi from the van on the mobile phone.'

On their way to the hospital Niccolo listened to the baby's heart with a foetal stethoscope, smiling at Jenny and giving a thumbs-up sign. Pauline saw that he had brought a sterile delivery pack and a portable incubator with an oxygen cylinder attached.

'We got a message that a baby was being born in

the street, so I thought I'd better be prepared,' he said in a low tone to Pauline, not adding that he had been about to go off duty when the call came through, but that there were no other doctors available. 'Tell me, Paolina, was that Enrico I saw standing with you?'

'Yes, it was he who telephoned,' she explained, thinking what a strange and providential reunion it had been, and remembering their first unfortunate encounter with Enrico. And to think that Niccolo took his turn at being one of those anonymous messengers of mercy in Florence!—it was yet another revelation about the mysterious Dr Ghiberti. . .

When Pauline got through to Riccardo on the mobile phone he said he would come straight to the hospital in a taxi; Jenny was speedily admitted to an antenatal ward, and a monitor was attached to her tummy to record any uterine contractions and the baby's heartbeat and movements. An obstetrician arrived to examine her, and made her lie on her left side and then on her right, then he sat her up and made her stand out of bed. A nurse carried out a test on the vaginal fluid, and reported that it was nitrazine negative, which meant that the waters around the baby were still intact.

'I think that the sciatic nerve has become inflamed, possibly due to the baby lying over it,' the obstetrician told Niccolo, who had already suspected something of the sort. 'The monitor shows some uterine irritability, but no real contractions,' he added, smiling at Jenny. 'We will keep you in with us overnight, *signora*, and may let you go tomorrow if you promise to take better care of yourself. No more dashing around the shops in all this heat!'

When Riccardo rushed in, Jenny burst into tears.

'Oh, Riccardo, I've upset everybody and frightened Pauline half to death, all for nothing!' she sobbed.

Pauline's relief was tinged with guilt because it was on her account that Jenny had been in the city. Not only that, but if Jenny had not collapsed in the street they would never have discovered Niccolo's secret membership of the Brotherhood. And there he was now, beckoning to her at the door of the ward.

'Paolina, I will take you back to the clinic, but first will you speak with me?' he asked her urgently.

She glanced back at Jenny, who was sitting up in bed with Riccardo bending over her.

'Your friend will be OK now, I think—please come with me,' Niccolo implored. She could hardly believe this change in her fortunes; she would have a chance to speak with him alone after all!

She smiled her assent, and he took her arm to lead her out of the hospital and down to the old city centre, where he turned towards the narrow street off which the Palazzo Alessandra lay.

'This way, Paolina.' He unlocked the iron gates into the pretty courtyard and led her up the outside stone steps to the first floor balcony. When she stepped towards the second flight, he caught her arm.

'No, *cara mia*, we will enter this unoccupied apartment.'

Putting a key into the door-lock, he opened it and stood back to let her pass into a passage from which two doors opened; one led to a kitchen, and one to a large and beautifully furnished *salotto*, with windows overlooking the city. Fine mahogany bookcases filled with leather-bound volumes occupied the whole of one wall, and a leather-topped escritoire with drawers and filing compartments gave the impression that the room had been used as a study. A globe stood in one corner, and a glass cabinet with a capital 'G' engraved on its central panel. Pauline remembered seeing the same decorated monogram in Annalisa's third-floor apartment. An idea began to form in her head, but it could be a coincidence that G stood for Ghiberti. . .

'Do you own this house, Niccolo?' she asked directly, turning to face him as he entered the room behind her and closed the door.

'Yes, since my parents died,' he answered sombrely. 'It has been in our family for more than two hundred years, but, having no family of my own, I have leased out the first and second floors to selected tenants, with Annalisa and her friends on the third floor.'

Pauline was quite shocked by this disclosure. 'Your *home*, Niccolo? Let out as flats to strangers?'

He shrugged. 'What other use can I make of the home where I was born, and where my sister and I grew up with our parents and house-servants? This was my father's room, and has been lately occupied by a research pathologist from Hamburg—a quiet man who needed a place to stay for six months.'

'I had no idea,' she said, shaking her head. 'Your childhood home!'

She remembered Jenny's talk of the proud Ghiberti family, and was struck by the sadness of their present situation. This graceful Florentine palace had been their home for generations, right up to when the tragic accident had made Niccolo the solitary male heir, with as yet no issue to carry on the tradition.

His voice cut in sharply on her reflections. 'You got my letter?'

She turned to him with reproach in her blue-grey eyes. 'Yes, Annalisa gave it to me. I could hardly believe that you—that you did not want to see me, Niccolo.'

As if unable to meet her eyes, he turned his head sharply away. 'How little you know,' he muttered under his breath.

'How can you say that?' she countered. 'All I know is that after everything—*everything* that has passed between us in the last two months—you did *not* want to see me, Niccolo. Not even to say goodbye.'

The words were out. Her voice trembled, but she had said what was on her mind and in her heart. His back was to her, and she felt that this was the time to leave. She began to walk quietly towards the door.

'No, Paolina. Wait—wait!' he ordered, moving quickly and putting out his arm to detain her.

'No, I've said what I—— Niccolo, let me go now! Niccolo! *O caro mio*. . .'

And then there were no more protests, no more words at all as he caught her in his arms and pulled her body towards him so sharply that she lost her footing and her head fell against his chest. His left arm encircled her and gripped her fiercely; his right hand pulled her head back so that his mouth could fasten upon hers with a consuming hunger, demanding a response. He could not even say her name, so deep and prolonged was their kiss, robbing them of breath; all previous inhibitions were now thrown to the winds, and he was unrestrained in his determination. With any other man in such a situation Pauline would have been afraid, but not with this man; she was ready to comply with his demand, to follow his lead.

When at length he released her and they stood panting, arms around each other's bodies, pressed so close that she could feel his probing hardness through the thin layers of clothing that separated them, she knew that her hour of destiny had come. She wanted him no less than he wanted her, and so she relaxed her limbs so that she might sink to the floor with him. . .

But he lifted her up in his arms and carried her through to the next room, where an enormous bed stood as if awaiting them. She was laid upon it, and immediately felt his long fingers undoing her dress, her bra loosened as the hook was freed. His eager lips were upon her throat, her shoulders, her breasts, her tummy as she lay in an agony of anticipation. A shiver ran through her whole body as he boldly searched for her woman's secret place, dark and moist. He whispered a question.

'*Tu mi ami, Paolina*?'

'*Si, Niccolo, ti amo. Ti amo!*' she replied, unafraid to declare her love.

It was all so easy, so simple, so natural when he entered her and claimed her as a lover. The incredible sensation of his body between her willingly opened thighs and the thrust of his proud spear deep within her, was a pleasure too strong to be taken in silence. Her low moans filled the room as his movements quickened, and she dug her fingers wildly into his dark hair; his head reared up above her as his climax approached and they both cried out together at the moment of his release. And in a glimpse of eternity Pauline knew an ecstasy such as she had never known before.

A warm river flowed, honouring her womanhood, and then they slowly descended down from the heights, their entwined limbs slackened, and they lay still like ships becalmed in a motionless sea. Pauline felt a delicious languor pervading her whole body and drifted off into a sweet sleep, clasped in her lover's arms.

After an immeasurable time his voice came to her, tender but insistent.

'Paolina, *cara*—we must wake now. It is past six.'

'What?' She opened her eyes and looked around the room, seeing for the first time the tapestry hangings, the matching window-seat and low padded stool beside the dressing-table.

'Niccolo——' She clung to him as he raised himself on one elbow to look down on her with a new possessiveness that made her spine tingle.

'*Mio tesoro*, we must leave now. They will need you back at the clinic, yes? Especially with the Signora Alberi in hospital.'

He reluctantly released himself from her arms and got off the bed. She gazed upon his male beauty—a living statue in the light that filtered through the half-closed shutters. Then reality returned with a rush, and she, too, sat up, shook her head and got off the bed. They both began to pick up their clothes and dress in silence; it was time for lovers to turn back into their everyday selves, though Pauline had difficulty in readjusting after the journey she had taken with Niccolo, which now appeared to have been quite out of this world.

But it was over now, and duties were calling.

After hurrying up the steep hill to Santa Maria Nuova, they found Jenny smiling and calm, and a very relieved Riccardo confirmed that she could return to the Clinico Silverio on the following day if no untoward symptoms occurred.

'I'm picking up the car and going back there now, Pauline, so you can come with me,' said Riccardo, nodding at Niccolo whom he knew was returning to England the next day.

He was clearly anxious to be off, and so, with a last wordlessly imploring look at the face of the man who had been all-in-all to her less than an hour ago, Pauline parted from him and left with Riccardo to collect the car and return to the clinic.

Niccolo stared at their retreating backs, and all at once clapped his right hand to his forehead in a gesture of dismay.

'May God forgive me—what have I done to that girl?' he asked himself under his breath as waves of regret began to wash over him.

CHAPTER TEN

PAULINE scarcely had time to think of Niccolo boarding the flight for Manchester as she did the rounds of her patients the following day—changing dressings and checking intravenous drips, persuading reluctant post-ops that to get out of bed and sit in an armchair for half an hour would not cause an irreversible relapse but would actually aid their recovery.

In addition to her responsibilities on the surgical suite, there was Jenny to care for on her return from hospital to her own double bed that she shared with her husband. Riccardo and Pauline were constantly on the alert for another crippling attack of the acute sciatic pain that had given them all such a fright. Carefully graduated exercises were worked out for Jenny by the visiting physiotherapist, and Riccardo absolutely forbade his wife to do any work at all, not even on Reception or in the accounts office.

Pauline was called upon more and more frequently to take charge of the clinic, and although she was a willing worker, and always welcomed a challenge, she found that she had hardly a minute to spare for herself. In her efforts to make the right decision over the many individual problems that occurred, she was anxious that no patient should be overlooked.

Annalisa still needed counselling and encouragement during her final week at the clinic, and although Nina was almost ready to face the outside world, her place was already virtually taken by a pitifully thin boy of eighteen, whose early film career had been brought to a standstill by the dreaded bulimia.

'He is going to need all the help we can give,' Sister Agnello pronounced with a heavenward glance.

So there was no time to brood, and it was only when Pauline lay down to sleep at the end of each well-occupied day that her thoughts were free to return to Niccolo. Then it was as if she lived in two worlds: on the one hand the Clinico Silverio, high up in the Tuscan hills, and on the other the tapestried walls and half-closed shutters of the first-floor bedroom in the Palazzo Alessandra, which had enclosed her and her Florentine lover in a magical world of love. Niccolo! Had he really held her in his arms and made her one with him? Indeed he had, and there was no doubting the depth of his desire for her, culminating in her joyous surrender and a perfect union of bodies and minds.

Niccolo, Niccolo, even if I do not see you again for many months—if not before next year—if not ever again—I shall live with that memory, she said in the silence of her heart as she looked up at the night sky and remembered every precious moment.

July came, and the temperature rose still higher. A letter arrived from Pauline's mother, asking why she had not written for so long, and happy news came from Vernio, where Giovanna and Stefano were rejoicing in their parenthood, freed from the shadows of depression.

Pauline had decided not to write to Niccolo until she had first heard from him, but ten days after his departure there was still no word. Then an envelope with his bold scrawl appeared in her pigeonhole at

Reception, and she eagerly tore it open, to find a single sheet.

My dear Paolina,

I feel so far away from you and from my home in Florence. Mr Mason is on holiday, so the senior registrar and I are holding the surgical team until he returns. You can imagine the demands on time and my imperfect knowledge of gastroenterology! I shall not forget the lessons I have gained from Annalisa's problems, nor what you taught me about differential diagnosis, dear Paolina.

You must guess my anxiety about you, my regret for my capitulation to selfishness—especially when you were so worried about Signora Alberi. I think that the Alberis have no great regard for me, but I am thankful that they are good friends to you.

Dear little Paolina, I beg you to let me know at once if you have any worries, though I trust you will suffer no effects. I cannot say more in this letter, which I write under difficulty in the lunch-hour.

Ti auguro la felicità—saluti affetuosi! Niccolo Ghiberti.

It could hardly be called a love letter, but Pauline felt that she understood his self-imposed restraint after the total abandonment of their last meeting. He was clearly still in favour of a period of reflection, and not keen to commit either of them to a definite understanding while they were so far apart. She saw the wisdom of this, she told herself, but. . .

She gave a little shiver, in spite of the heat. Was he already regretting their mutual declaration of love?

Had he actually said that he loved her? She could not remember. *She* had said, '*Ti amo*', but had he? There had been no talk of marriage. There had been very little talk at all. . .

She wrote him an affectionate but non-committal letter in the same strain, telling him that Annalisa was coping well back in the apartment with Maria and Elena. She also wrote that Nina had weighed fifty-four kilograms—eight and a half stone—on discharge, and shared with him the happy news of the Sandrinis.

'I have no regrets at all about what happened in your home,' she wrote in the final paragraph. 'Therefore there is no need for you to reproach yourself. Write to me when you have time, though I know that you are very busy during Mr Mason's absence.'

She pondered for a while on how she should end the letter, and decided to follow his example and put 'I wish you happiness'—but should it be 'Pauline Stephens'? She finally penned the single word, 'Paolina'.

July passed in breathless heat, and Jenny's blood pressure began to rise. Pauline noted her swollen legs and ankles with disquiet, and tried to make her rest more, but, even lying on the sun-bed in the shade, Jenny said it was difficult to find a comfortable position. Riccardo became irritable through worry and lack of sleep due to Jenny's restlessness and walking about at night, so Pauline needed all her natural tact and optimism to guide the expectant couple through the final stages of waiting.

Then, on the second day of August, an auxiliary nurse came running to Pauline's room at four o'clock in the morning with an urgent summons to attend the *signora* at once. Hastily throwing on her dressing-gown, Pauline rushed to the Alberis' room where she found the bed soaked and Jenny gasping with discomfort as her tummy tightened rhythmically with unmistakable uterine contractions. She had gone into spontaneous labour with rupture of the membranes just one month before the expected date of delivery.

'She contracts strongly, Pauline!' exclaimed Riccardo with a worried frown. 'I telephone for an ambulance to take her to Santa Maria Nuova, yes? Better not go in the car, no?'

Pauline smiled. Dr Alberi was no different from any other nervous expectant father. He rarely encountered obstetric patients at the clinic, and obviously doubted his own competence to deal with a premature birth.

'Wait a minute, Riccardo—Jenny might be better staying here,' she said quietly. 'The baby's a good enough size, but it could come quickly. Hand me the foetal stethoscope to check its heartbeat, and then I'll do a vaginal examination to see how far on she is before we make a decision.' Pauline had no wish whatever for an ambulance delivery.

The baby's heartbeat proved to be strong and regular, and when Pauline did an examination she found the cervix already half-dilated at five centimetres; the contractions were rapidly becoming stronger and closer together, so a pain-relieving injection of pethidine was checked by Riccardo and given by Pauline into Jenny's buttock.

'There you go, love, it will ease the height of the pain for you and help you to relax,' she reassured her friend, feeling reasonably confident that speedy progress would be made.

In this she was justified, because the pethidine

proved effective. While Jenny dozed intermittently the cervix continued to dilate steadily, and, after quickly dressing in her uniform, Pauline occupied herself in preparing the cot and seeing that everything was ready for the delivery. She felt exhilarated at the prospect of a home confinement in ideal conditions, and she mentally set aside a certain personal dilemma of her own, now almost certainly confirmed.

Just before seven Jenny stirred and gave a cry of alarm.

'Pauline, quick, I need the toilet—help me to get there!' she begged in embarrassment.

'Shh, love, I don't think you do,' soothed Pauline. 'I'm pretty sure that it's the baby's head you can feel. Let me just see now—good girl. Don't worry, everything's just fine.'

'Help! I want to push,' wailed Jenny as Riccardo rushed to her side. 'I can't stop myself!'

Pauline set to work, getting her friend to take deep breaths from the face-mask attached to the gas and oxygen cylinder, and to push down when a contraction came on. In another twenty minutes the birth was imminent, and Pauline made an episiotomy incision to ensure a wider outlet and easier passage for a smaller than average baby. While Jenny panted and Riccardo murmured words of loving encouragement Pauline skilfully manoeuvred a curly little head through the last phase of its journey and into the light of day. The rest of the body followed swiftly, and a healthy baby girl lay between Jenny's legs, filling the room with her piercing cries. Her parents wept for joy, and Pauline heaved a huge sigh of relief.

Lucia Alberi weighed in at two point eight kilograms, or six pounds and two ounces, and Pauline pronounced her perfect in every way. The proud parents, calling each other *mamma* and *babbo*, held their daughter while Pauline supervised the expulsion of the placenta. There was no significant blood loss, and Pauline was glad that she had learned to suture episiotomies at Beltonshaw General. Riccardo assisted her, admiring her technique at stitching together the layers of muscle and delicate skin.

An excited auxiliary was sent to prepare a tray of tea for the new mother and the midwife, and the news soon spread throughout the Clinico Silverio.

'Thank you, dearest Pauline, you've been simply marvellous,' sighed Jenny, holding her friend in a grateful embrace. 'I'm so glad that you were here to deliver our darling Lucia.' Riccardo also added his heartfelt thanks, kissing Pauline on both cheeks, Italian-style.

Pauline smiled and assured them that she felt honoured to share in the joy of Lucia's birth, and she was pleased to see the baby sucking away eagerly at her first breast-feed.

'I'll leave you two alone with her for a little while, to get acquainted,' she told them. 'I'll be in the bathroom if you need me, OK?'

When she had closed the door, and was alone with her thoughts, Pauline burst into tears in an overflowing of emotion; and it was not only due to reaction after the past four hours.

It was because she now faced the fact that she too was to have a child, in March of the following year.

Jenny and Riccardo were taken aback but immediately sympathetic when they heard her news.

'You must tell Dr Ghiberti, of course, Pauline, love,'

said Jenny. 'And don't worry about a thing. We'll look after you, just as you've looked after me. It'll be our pleasure!'

'Yes, Pauline, you will have your baby here with us—we shall help you through everything, yes?' added Riccardo comfortingly.

They both seemed to assume that Niccolo might not be willing to shoulder his responsibilities, but Pauline suspected that they wanted to put her mind at ease, just in case she met with an unsatisfactory response from her child's father.

After careful thought she decided not to write to Niccolo but to tell him personally when she went home for her mother's wedding on September the second. With Jenny safely delivered, this was no longer a problem, and Pauline now began to count the days to her booked flight on August the twenty-eighth.

Another letter had arrived from Niccolo, which had hardly been reassuring, as he had written of his 'great relief' to hear that Pauline was well, and that there was 'no need for worry' about her. His meaning was obvious, and Pauline trembled at the thought of having to disillusion him when they met in Beltonshaw. How should she set about it? she wondered. Should she write, or telephone him at the hospital to arrange a meeting? And, if so, where? She both longed for that moment and dreaded it.

And yet. . .the knowledge that she carried Niccolo Ghiberti's child was a matter for joy, whatever his reaction might be. With the support of the Alberis, who were like a brother and sister to her, she was confident that she could cope with life as a single mother if that was to be her fate.

*   *   *

Pauline had underestimated the natural perception of her own mother, however. Helen Stephens met her at Manchester Airport, and they got a taxi to Belthonshaw.

'Graham wanted to bring me in the car, but I felt we needed to be on our own at this first meeting after so long,' explained Helen, and Pauline appreciated her mother's sensitivity.

It was strange to see the 'SOLD' notice on their semi-detached home, Dr Stafford owned a large detached house into which he would welcome his new bride.

'It's a bit big for the two of us, really, and I've wondered if we could convert the top floor into a self-contained flat for a junior partner, or even a doctor from Beltonshaw General,' confided Helen happily. 'But never mind about that now—I want to hear all about life in Florence. Your letters have been rather short and scrappy of late, Pauline!'

Her daughter laughed and apologised. 'It's just that life has been so unbelievably hectic, Mum! If I were to tell you everything that's happened since I set foot in Italy——'

She stopped, suddenly aware of the look in her mother's eyes. She saw love, concern—and knowledge.

'You don't need to tell me everything, Pauline, but there is something that you'll *have* to tell me, isn't there?' prompted Mrs Stephens gently.

'Oh, Mum—how did you know?' asked Pauline as Helen held out her arms. 'It's only ten weeks. . .'

Her mother sighed and held her close.

'It will be that Italian doctor who came over here and then went back to Florence because of his sister,' she said.

'Yes, you're right; it's Niccolo. And he's back here again now,' whispered Pauline. 'I'm going to tell him, but not until after your wedding. Oh, Mum, I love him so!'

'I know you do, dear,' replied Helen gravely. 'Your letters left me in no doubt of that. And I'm prepared to love him, too, as a son. But you say he doesn't even *know*?'

'No, not yet. It was just the once, you see. The very day before he left for Manchester in June.'

Helen's face was more stern now. 'He should be told without any further delay, Pauline. Couldn't you have written to him?'

'I want to tell him personally,' pleaded Pauline.

'My dear, the sooner this doctor faces up to his duty, the better,' her mother stated firmly. 'Would you like me to ask Graham to have a word with him?'

'Good heavens, no!' cried Pauline in horror. 'Oh, please don't worry, Mum. I'll see him and tell him as soon as your wedding's over. Will there be a lot of doctors coming?' she asked, in an effort to steer the conversation in another direction.

'Quite a few, including Mr Mason the consultant surgeon, who's an old friend of Graham's,' replied her mother. 'He's actually agreed to be best man!' She paused, then went on, 'I seem to remember that Dr—er, Niccolo?—was working on his team.'

'Yes, he still is,' replied Pauline with a sinking heart. 'Oh, Mum, I don't want to cause you and Graham any trouble at all! If by any chance Niccolo—— I mean, if for *any* reason we don't get married, I shall go back to the Clinico Silverio and have the baby there. Jenny and Riccardo are the most wonderful friends in the world, and they've promised to take care of me. So, whatever happens, I'll be just fine—honestly. You mustn't let this spoil your wedding!'

She was so agitated that her mother suggested a cup of tea and pretended to be satisfied with Pauline's assurances.

But privately Helen Stephens was not in the least bit satisfied, and had no intention of letting this Italian doctor duck his responsibilities. She spoke to her fiancé that night, and together they hatched a plan to ensure that if Niccolo Ghiberti accepted his duty he would be publicly welcomed into the family. However, if he did not, the whole medical fraternity of Beltonshaw would know of his treachery—including Mr Mason.

St Antony's Church was packed to capacity when the bride stepped out of the wedding-car, accompanied by her brother, who was to give her away, and her two little granddaughters who were bridesmaids. Helen looked charming in a pearl-grey silk dress and jacket, with a picture hat framing her soft grey curls. Its brim turned up at the front to allow her smiles to be seen by the many relatives and friends who had come to the wedding of a widely respected Beltonshaw family doctor.

Inside the church Pauline sat with her elder sister and brother-in-law, the parents of the bridesmaids. Her face was pale, and she found the crowded pews and rich floral fragrances rather oppressive. Having so far avoided morning sickness, she felt nauseated for the first time, and had taken no breakfast. Her heart thumped as the organ sounded and the congregation stood to greet the bride now beginning her stately progress up the aisle.

The printed order of service trembled in Pauline's hands, and all at once a sickening sensation of doubt and apprehension filled her. She became aware of the vulnerability of her situation as an unmarried pregnant woman with a lifetime of motherhood ahead. How would her career be affected if she had to support her child? Where would she live after its birth—in Italy? Or would she return to England? Thoughts of financial and legal issues rose up to distress her. What if she became ill? What if——?

The bride had now reached the altar rail and was smiling at her groom, who stood waiting with his old friend. The strains of the organ rose up to the vaulted roof, but to Pauline the music sounded like ominous peals of thunder crashing round her. A sense of panic seized her throat, and she could not draw breath; she swayed against her sister, who put out an arm to support her, while at that very moment there occurred a totally unexpected disturbance in the church.

From the west door a man dashed up the aisle, obviously searching for someone. His dark eyes frantically scanned the front pews, and he gave an audible exclamation as they alighted on the one he sought. Pushing his way along the pew and muttering, '*Mi scusi—mi scusi, grazie*,' the latecomer stumbled to his place beside Pauline.

'Shh!' came a murmur of annoyance from around them as smartly dressed guests craned their heads to see the bride and groom standing before the priest.

'Paolina! O, Paolina, cara mia. *Perché non mi l'hai detto*?' he asked with deep reproach. 'Why did you not tell me?'

'Shh!' repeated the voices as he clasped the half fainting woman in his arms. There were tears in his eyes as he kissed her white face and begged her to forgive him.

'*Ti amo. Ti amo, Paolina. Mi perdoni ti prego*!'

Pauline's sister stared in astonishment at the tall

stranger, and the rustlings and murmurings all around them subsided as the guests became aware of a high drama being enacted among the bride's relatives. Whispers were passed along the rows in front and behind, and significant glances exchanged.

Pauline felt her drooping spirits revive in the warmth of Niccolo's presence. She had no idea why he had suddenly appeared beside her, as if in response to her need; the overwhelming fact that he was *here* was all that mattered. Her colour returned and she stood up straight beside him as the wedding service proceeded.

'*Perché*—why have you not told me, Paolina?' he repeated again.

'Shh!' she answered, smiling and holding a finger to her lips. With that he had to be content, though he kissed her again, and could not take his eyes from her. The lovers were reunited, never again to be parted.

And Dr Niccolo Ghiberti had passed the test set for him by his future mother-in-law and her husband of today.

He had been chatting with two nurses in the office of the male surgical ward at midday on that sunny first Saturday of September. There were no clinics or operating lists at the weekend, and, apart from an emergency appendicectomy the night before, there had been no urgent problems. The surgical team had been headed by the senior registrar that day, because Mr Mason was attending a wedding, and the atmosphere had been generally relaxed.

Until the junior houseman had strolled into the office and winked at the pretty staff nurse at the desk.

'Dr Ghiberti, have I got news for you!' he had announced. 'You're to take the rest of the day off—special message from the great man himself!'

'What is this?' asked Niccolo, suspecting a joke. 'Mr Mason has gone to a wedding today!'

'You're right there, *Dottore*—he has, indeed.' The houseman grinned, thoroughly enjoying himself. 'And *you* have to go too, on a last-minute invitation from the happy bridegroom—Dr Stafford!'

Niccolo frowned and spread out his hands. 'You pull my leg, Doctor! I do not know this Dr Stafford. Why should Mr Mason require that I attend the wedding of a stranger?'

'You'd better believe it, Ghiberti, or you could be in dead trouble,' said the young doctor more seriously, gesturing to the nurses not to giggle. 'And you'd better get a move on—it starts at two. St Antony's—not very far to go, but I'd get a taxi lined up if I were you. Have you got anything to wear?'

Niccolo did not rise from his chair. 'If you are trying to make me look a fool, Doctor——'

'You'll look a worse fool if you don't move yourself, Ghiberti,' the houseman replied, with a glance at the open-mouthed nurses. 'This Dr Stafford has got a very good reason for wanting you there. I'm not joking—this is for real. Mr Mason's waiting for you, and if you don't show up——'

'I tell you, Doctor, I do not know this Dr Stafford!' protested Niccolo in utter bewilderment.

'Maybe not, but—er—from what I've heard——' the houseman leaned towards his superior and lowered his voice '—you know his bride's daughter. Rather well, so I gather. You know how hospital gossip whizzes along the grapevine.'

He stopped speaking as Niccolo's eyes stared in horror and the colour visibly drained from his face. His mouth dropped open as he remembered Pauline telling him her mother's news back in March. He had asssumed then that the marriage was to take place very soon.

'Is—is this Dr Stafford marrying a lady called—Mrs Stephens?' he croaked in a voice not his own.

'Could be—I think that's the name,' answered the houseman. 'And if hospital rumours are anything to go by, there'll have to be another wedding pretty soon for her daughter. And *you'll* have to be *there*, old son!' he added, with a forthright lack of respect that convinced his hearers more than any sworn protestations of truth.

One moment Ghiberti was sitting on a chair, the next he had vanished, leaving the junior doctor to shrug at the nurses, who stared at him and at each other.

'I don't believe it!' exclaimed the pretty staff nurse.

'Time will show,' muttered the houseman, not sorry to have given the haughty Italian registrar the shock of his life.

The wedding-reception was held in the banqueting suite of Beltonshaw's largest hotel. A happy if rather unusual encounter took place when the bride's daughter presented her fiancé of an hour to her mother and newly married stepfather. Kisses and handshakes followed, and Niccolo was properly introduced to Pauline's sister and her family. He found himself the focus of much speculation—especially when Mr Mason kissed Pauline and introduced her and Niccolo to his wife.

As the lovers stood together holding their glasses—his filled with champagne, hers with orange juice—they had eyes only for each other.

'I had not intended it to be like this, Paolina,'

Niccolo told her. 'I had hoped for a big Ghiberti wedding next summer, when I would show you to all my relatives and friends in Tuscany—but now that fate has stepped in I see it as the best thing that could happen, yes?' He smiled, raptly gazing down upon her upturned face. 'We shall ask the same priest to marry us in this same Sant' Antonio as soon as he can, and I must find somewhere for us to live while I finish my exchange year.'

Pauline remembered what her mother had said about converting Dr Stafford's top floor into a flat.

'I think I know the very place for us, where I can be close to my mother and still have privacy with you,' she told him with shining eyes, and was about to explain when a thought suddenly struck her. 'Oh, dear! I shall have to tell Jenny and Riccardo that I shan't be returning to Florence after all!'

'Not yet, little Paolina, not yet! First we have to look forward to the spring, and the birth of a little baby to Signora Ghiberti, yes?'

His eyes melted with adoration for her as they stood among the milling guests, and, seizing her free hand, he held it against his heart.

'*E dopo, amore mio, andremo a Firenze con il nostro bambino*!' Pauline's heart soared at the prospect of returning to Florence—her city of destiny—with their newborn baby—which Niccolo seemed to assume would be a boy. Once again there would be a proper Ghiberti family in the Palazzo Alesssandra—*and* room for Annalisa on the top floor!

'*Si, Niccolo*,' she answered softly. '*Alla città del mio destino*.'

And, oblivious of the smiling onlookers, the lovers sealed their promise with a kiss.

GET 4 BOOKS AND A MYSTERY GIFT

Return this coupon and we'll send you 4 Love on Call novels and a mystery gift absolutely FREE! We'll even pay the postage and packing for you.

We're making you this offer to introduce you to the benefits of Reader Service: FREE home delivery of brand-new Love on Call novels, at least a month before they are available in the shops, FREE gifts and a monthly Newsletter packed with information.

Accepting these FREE books and gift places you under no obligation to buy, you may cancel at any time, even after receiving just your free shipment. Simply complete the coupon below and send it to:

MILLS & BOON READER SERVICE, FREEPOST, CROYDON, SURREY, CR9 3WZ.

No stamp needed

Yes, please send me 4 free Love on Call novels and a mystery gift. I understand that unless you hear from me, I will receive 4 superb new titles every month for just £1.99* each postage and packing free. I am under no obligation to purchase any books and I may cancel or suspend my subscription at any time, but the free books and gifts will be mine to keep in any case. (I am over 18 years of age)

1EP6D

Ms/Mrs/Miss/Mr _____

Address _____

_____

_____ Postcode _____

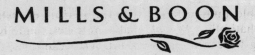

MILLS & BOON

LOVE CALL

The books for enjoyment this month are:

PRESCRIPTION FOR CHANGE	Sheila Danton
REMEDY FOR PRIDE	Margaret Holt
TOTAL RECALL	Laura MacDonald
PRACTICE IN THE CLOUDS	Meredith Webber

Treats in store!

Watch next month for the following absorbing stories:

A FRESH DIAGNOSIS	Jessica Matthews
BOUND BY HONOUR	Josie Metcalfe
UNEXPECTED COMPLICATIONS	Joanna Neil
CRUISE DOCTOR	Stella Whitelaw